"Do you think I'm pretending with you?"

Emma couldn't evade his question. "What else?" she said. "It's second nature to you, Jake. Celia Manners arrives tomorrow, and you'll be doing the same with her."

"Purely business. It won't mean anything."

Emma longed to hit him. "I don't mean anything to you, either. No woman does. You're too scared of commitments."

"Perhaps you could make me change my mind," Jake ventured softly, his expression oddly serious. "You're intelligent, humorous and honest—a rare combination. I'd enjoy teaching you about love."

"I'm sure," Emma retorted. "But could you *love* me, apart from merely wanting me?"

The warmth evaporated, leaving Jake's face a hard cold mask.

KAY CLIFFORD
is also the author of this
Harlequin Romance

2468—NO TIME FOR LOVE

Many of these titles are available at your local bookseller.

For a free catalog listing all titles currently available,
send your name and address to:

A Temporary Affair

by

KAY CLIFFORD

Harlequin Books

TORONTO • NEW YORK • LOS ANGELES • LONDON
AMSTERDAM • PARIS • SYDNEY • HAMBURG
STOCKHOLM • ATHENS • TOKYO • MILAN

Original hardcover edition published in 1982
by Mills & Boon Limited

ISBN 0-373-02505-X

Harlequin Romance first edition October 1982

To
my darling Michael, with whom
I've had a very permanent affair!

Printed in U.S.A.

CHAPTER ONE

Emma Porter fastened her safety belt and tried to relax as the Boeing 737 revved its engines for take-off. As she had never flown before, her excitement was tinged with nervousness as the huge plane left the runway, but within a few minutes the thrill of finally being on her way to Majorca made her forget her apprehension, and she settled back to enjoy the flight.

It was only as the stewardess distributed the daily papers that the butterflies returned. Glimpsing a copy of *The Times* reminded her again of her family's warning that she was courting trouble by accepting a job about which she knew so little. But it was too late to change her mind. Her decision, made in haste, to cook for a household of gourmets would leave little time for her to repent at leisure.

But for the next couple of hours at least, she had leisure in plenty, and her fears grew as she wondered how she would cope in the months ahead.

Over the rubbery chicken and limp salad that passed for dinner, they hit an air-pocket, and Emma immediately forgot her job in the more pressing need not to lose what she had just eaten. Unfortunately it was a lost battle, and by the time the turbulence had subsided, she both looked and felt considerably the worse for wear.

Shakily making her way to the toilet, she washed her wan face and attempted to remove some of the stains from her badly crumpled dress. What a mess she looked! Her normally bouncy hair—rich brown in colour—hung lankly over her shoulders, and although she brushed it vigorously, the sheen refused to return.

Plucking off her pink-framed glasses, she peered myopically at her eyes. Widely spaced, and hazel in colour, they were her best feature, though they did not look it now, for they were ringed by smudged mascara that had streaked from her lashes. Despite her rubbing frantically at them with a dampened tissue, it was impossible to remove all the smearing without a proper cleanser. Annoyingly the waterproofing lived up to its boast and she looked even more like a panda than before!

Re-applying lipstick to her small, pert mouth, she wished for the millionth time that she was half a head taller; how impossible it was to look confident and assured if one were only five feet one. With a sigh, she smoothed her kaftan over her hips. Its loose style gave no hint of the perfectly proportioned body it covered, nor did the material itself do anything for her. Something more vivid than muted browns would have been more flattering to her olive complexion, but the imperious saleslady at Harrods had managed to convince her otherwise.

As she returned to her seat, Emma's companion—an elderly woman called Mrs Grant—regarded her kindly. 'You look much better now, my dear.'

'I wish I felt it,' Emma grimaced. 'I could do with a bath and a change of clothes.'

'You'll be in Paguera within an hour or so of landing,' Mrs Grant replied consolingly.

Ten minutes later they touched down at Palma Airport. It was nine-thirty, and all Emma could see of the town were the lights twinkling prettily against a sky glowing like black satin in the moonlight.

Her companion's burly, suntanned husband greeted his wife as she and Emma cleared Customs together, and as he went to steer her towards the exit, Mrs Grant looked at Emma with concern.

'Are you sure you'll be all right on your own? Perhaps you'd like us to stay with you until you're collected?'

'It's very kind of you, but there's no need. I'm sure I won't have to wait very long.' Emma glanced hopefully around the crowded room, but no one made a move towards her.

Within a moment the Grants disappeared from view as more passengers surged through the arrival hall. The heat generated by the crowd became intense, and Emma learned from a fellow traveller that the air-conditioning had broken down.

No wonder her skin was shiny with perspiration and her glasses kept slipping down her nose! If only she had had the sense to wear her contact lenses; it would at least have made her appearance more prepossessing. But her lenses were new, and unless she was completely relaxed they did not feel comfortable.

An hour later Emma was still waiting to be collected, seated on a hard plastic-covered bench with her cases at her feet. She walked outside to cool off, but the steamy night air seemed little different from inside. She was beginning to feel afraid that the Sanders had misunderstood the time of her arrival. When she had telephoned the house from England, none of the family had been at home, and she had left a message with the Spanish maid, whose English was far from fluent. She would wait another hour and see: if no one arrived to meet the next plane from Heathrow, she would take a taxi to Paguera.

Tired and irritated, she sat down again. The airport was less crowded now, as flights were not as frequent at this time of night, and her glance caught that of a bearded young man whom she had not previously noticed. He was standing several feet away, smoking a cheroot and lazily studying every attractive woman who went by. His piercing blue eyes, set beneath thick, dark blond brows, studied her deliberately, and after looking her up and down as if he were mentally undressing her, shifted away—making her even more aware of her forlorn appearance.

He was not exactly a picture of sartorial elegance himself, she decided, eyeing his worn blue jeans cut off at the knees. But he was incredibly handsome. In fact the word beautiful would have sprung to mind if his Viking-like build had not refuted that adjective as being too feminine. His thick mop of blond hair, several shades lighter than his beard and eyebrows, was brushed casually back from a high forehead, and in profile, as he turned away from her to eye another pretty girl, she saw that his nose was perfectly straight. He must have been about six feet, but his long lean legs, clad in their improvised shorts, made him appear even taller.

As if tired of standing, he shuffled his dusty feet in their open-toed leather sandals and let his eyes roam again in her direction. She hastily averted her own, not wanting him to catch her studying him. It would be awful if he mistook her curiosity and thought she were trying to pick him up! He was probably on the look-out for rich unattached females—and with his looks there would be no shortage of takers. That was probably why he had dismissed her so quickly—but if nothing better arrived, he might turn his attention in her direction.

Hurriedly she rose and wandered to the exit once again. Her grandparents had not wanted her to come here, and she began to wish she had taken their advice. Old-fashioned though they were, they had her best interests at heart, and had been devoted surrogate parents since her own had been killed in a motorway accident ten years ago.

Her father had been their only child and they had tended to coddle her, afraid she might be taken from them too. Though they had sent her to boarding school, they put up tremendous opposition to any mention of her leaving home and finding a job, and she had had to fight determinedly before being allowed to take a cookery course in London. Even then they had only agreed because they felt cookery to be a necessary requisite for a marriageable young lady, but had insisted she live under the strict supervision of some elderly, childless relatives.

After she had graduated with honours, Emma's desire to remain in London had suffered a temporary setback when her grandmother became ill, and she had felt duty bound to return home. Since she had believed it would only be for a few weeks, her affectionate nature had been no match for her grandmother's subtle play on her loyalty, and the weeks became months, and the months a complete year. True, she had found herself a job in the village library, but it did not utilise her training, and she knew the time would come when she would have to make a stand for herself, or give in to her grandparents completely and live her life as *they* wished it.

'I can't understand why you have to work at all,' her grandmother said one afternoon when Emma returned from the library fuming at the high-handed behaviour of Miss Ambrose, the head librarian, who tended to treat her as if she were eleven and not twenty-one. 'In my day, girls were quite content to stay home until they married.'

'I might not marry for years,' Emma replied.

Her grandmother looked at her sharply. 'I thought it was all settled between you and Peter.'

'Not as far as I'm concerned. I haven't made a final decision yet.'

'Don't delay too long, my dear. We won't be here for ever, and our dearest wish is to see you happily married. Peter's a charming boy, and will do everything he can to make you happy.'

'By which you mean that he's lucky enough to be a

solicitor in his father's firm,' Emma quipped. 'But I want more than security, Grandma. I want excitement and fun and romance.'

'Then watch television!' her grandmother retorted, 'and count yourself lucky Peter has patience with you.'

But Emma was determined not to be pressured by her grandparents' continual hints for her to set their minds at ease. She loved them deeply and was mindful of all they had done for her, but marriage—for her—would be a lifetime's commitment, and she was going to make up her own mind.

The trouble was, it was easier to give in to people you loved than to fight them. But she knew that unless she made an effort and refused to be swayed by her grandmother's clinging attitude, she would never have a chance to know what she could do or what her potential was.

However, it was not until Peter proposed for the third time that she realised she had to leave Oakton. If she remained, she would inevitably find herself accepting him.

'I thought I'd look for a job abroad for a few months in the summer,' she told her grandparents over coffee the following evening, and waited with apprehension for the storm of protest that would follow.

'Doing what?' her grandfather demanded.

'Cooking, or looking after children. I hadn't really thought.'

'Don't be a silly child!' Her grandmother's lips tightened. 'You know how we feel about you leaving home.'

'I do,' Emma sighed, 'but it will only be for a short while. Apart from school trips, I've never travelled anywhere.'

'You'll have plenty of time for that when you're married.'

Emma forced herself to say nothing and reached for

The Times, which her grandfather was no longer reading. Idly she browsed through it, then turned to the situations vacant column. Almost immediately her eyes were drawn to an advertisement set out in a large box. It sounded ideal.

'Experienced cook wanted for gourmet household in luxury villa Majorca, July, August and September. Driving essential. Own room and bathroom. Other help kept. Wages £60 per week clear. Return fare paid. Write giving full details of experience, age + photograph. Sanders, Villa Marquesa, Paguera, Majorca.'

'I've found something!' she cried excitedly, and read it out aloud.

'I think you'd be most unwise to go abroad to work for people you don't know,' her grandmother warned. 'You've never had a full-time job and I'm sure you won't like taking orders.'

'I take orders at the library. Miss Ambrose can be an old martinet when the mood takes her.'

'Peter won't approve of you going away,' her grandfather added.

'That certainly won't stop me,' Emma asserted. 'Before I agree to marry him I have to make sure it's what I want. This will give me time to think things over.'

'You're a foolish girl,' her grandmother said sharply. 'Peter's a dear boy and you won't do better.'

With an effort, Emma curbed her irritation. 'I'd still like to try for this job. Three months with pay in the sun can't be bad.'

'If you're short of money you have only to ask us,' her grandfather retorted.

'I'm not. I save nearly all my allowance as it is. I just want to be completely independent for a while. Can't you please try to understand?'

It was obvious that they didn't, but they put up no

further opposition, understanding by the set look on Emma's face that her mind was made up.

She immediately sat down and wrote a long letter to Mrs Sanders, giving details of her training. She knew she was not an ideal choice—her inexperience would count against her—but if they did not receive a more suitable applicant, she hoped her enthusiasm would be compensation enough. Not giving herself time for second thoughts overnight, she ran out and posted the letter as soon as it was finished. She was intelligent enough to realise that three months in Majorca would not solve her problems. But she had to get away from the stifling, pampered atmosphere at home, and this could be the start of her independence.

Four weeks went by and Emma had given up all hope of receiving an answer to her letter, when one finally came. Heart pounding, she stared at the pale blue envelope, then hastily tore it open. A thin slip of typewritten paper fluttered out.

'Accept your application', read the note. 'Phone time and date of arrival for collection at airport. Reverse charges.' Beneath this brief acknowledgment came the barely decipherable signature, 'Jane Sanders', and below it a scrawled telephone number.

Emma bit back her disappointment. Although she was delighted at getting the job, the letter was terse and unfriendly, completely ignoring all her own queries. She nibbled worriedly at her lower lip, uncertain what to do. But her grandparents' tight-lipped disapproval when she showed them the reply served to increase her determination to accept—in spite of her own misgivings—as did Peter's annoyance when he took her out that evening and she broke the news to him.

'You should have discussed it with me before you did anything,' he said crossly. 'After all, we *are* engaged.'

'Not officially.'

'And whose fault is that? You know I want to marry you.'

If only she could tell him that was the reason she was leaving! But desire to avoid an argument kept her silent.

Instead she studied him as he refilled her glass of wine. He was a pleasant enough looking young man, slim, with sandy coloured hair which had started to recede slightly at the front, although he had not yet turned thirty. Emma had known him since she had come to live in Oakton as a young girl, but for the past year, since returning from London, he had been her steady boy-friend. It was her inexperience with other men more than anything else that made her hesitate to accept his proposal. How could she possibly know if he was right for her when she had never been out for any length of time with anyone else?

Living with elderly relations in London while studying at cookery school had provided her with little opportunity for meeting young people. The girls in her class were too snobbish and sophisticated for her taste, and her best friend had been a young teacher at the school with a similar background to her own. Occasionally she had been asked to parties—sensing it was only because there was a shortage of girls—and had found the easy-going sexual attitudes so different from her own that she had felt uncomfortable and naïve. But it was not a naïvety of which she was ashamed—on the contrary—and she had gradually opted out of the social scene and spent most of her time in galleries and concert halls. Once she had her diploma and a job, she would start to do something about her social life.

Unfortunately, because of her grandmother's illness, things had not turned out as she had planned, and here she was, a year later, just about to try her wings—and her cookery expertise. It was a scaring thought.

Emma jumped as she heard a Spanish voice announcing the arrival of the eleven o'clock flight from Heathrow. Absorbed in her reminiscences, she had not noticed the time. She stood up and hopefully looked around, but fifteen minutes later, when the last passenger had emerged and been greeted, there was still no one to meet her.

With a case in each hand she staggered towards the telephone kiosk. The instructions were written in English as well as Spanish, and putting the correct amount of pesetas in the slot, she dialled the Sanders' number. There was no reply, and after the tenth ring, she put down the receiver and forlornly made her way to the exit.

Outside stood a fleet of taxis of varying makes, headed by a white Mercedes coupé, its black hood lowered in the warm night air. Leaning against it was the bearded young man.

He bent to adjust one of the wing mirrors, and the muscles of his powerful chest rippled beneath his white singlet as he moved. Apparently he had not been successful in picking up someone tonight, although if his car was anything to go by, being a gigolo combined with driving a taxi and fleecing the tourists was a lucrative proposition. Emma would have preferred to approach one of the other drivers, but as he headed the line, she had no choice but to approach him.

Hesitatingly she showed him the piece of paper and addressed him in slow, carefully enunciated English. 'You . . . drive . . . me . . . to Paguera?'

A slight smile curved his full lips as he took the paper out of her hand. But as he saw the address, this changed to a look of astonishment, and instead of replying, he frowned and bit his lip.

Deciding he had not understood her request, she repeated it. '*Por favor,*' she began with a smile to mask her nervousness, while frantically praying that the only two words she knew in Spanish might establish a friendly rapport. 'You . . . drive . . . me . . . to Paguera?'

'Who the hell are *you*?' came the surprise response in perfect English.

She was so taken aback by his question that she was momentarily speechless.

'Well, answer me,' he said.

'I haven't the faintest idea what you're talking about,' she replied, with as much dignity as she could muster.

He ran long, ink-stained fingers through his hair, mussing it carelessly as he shook his head in puzzlement.

'Then I'll ask you again—who are you, and what are you doing with this address?'

Emma had just about had enough. 'If you don't want to take me there, say so. But I don't think it's necessary for me to give you my life history.'

'From the look of you, that wouldn't be very interesting,' he said rudely. 'I'm only curious to know how you happen to have this address.'

'I'm here to work as a cook for the family,' she said distantly.

'Impossible!'

'I can show you my letter of acceptance if you like. Although what business it is of yours. . . .'

'It's very much my business. There's been one hell of a mix-up if what you say is true. I've been waiting to meet the cook for the past two hours, but I certainly didn't expect *you*. If——'

Emma did not give him a chance to say any more. Overcome as she was by tiredness and worry, her normal reticence disappeared and she turned on him in a fury.

'Surely you were given my photograph?' she snapped. 'I haven't changed since it was taken. But then you were so busy eyeing every other girl in the place that I'm not surprised you didn't recognise *me*.'

'Nor am I,' he answered insolently, and taking a small picture from the pocket of his shorts, flashed it in front of her. 'You look quite different without your moustache!'

She snatched the photograph from his hand and found herself staring at a middle-aged man sporting a bushy moustache. Feeling rather foolish at her outburst, she handed it back. 'There certainly has been a mix-up,' she murmured. 'Mrs Sanders must have given you the wrong snapshot.'

'*Mrs* Sanders?' he repeated, puzzled.

'Jane Sanders—your employer,' Emma said slowly, wondering how she was ever going to make him understand.

'Considering that we both speak the same language we're having a hell of a difficult time communicating,' he remarked coldly. 'There is no Mrs Sanders—at least not on this island, as far as I know. But there is a Mr Sanders and he did engage a cook—but a male one,' he waggled the photograph. 'Not a female.'

'I see.' Emma did, and was dismayed. 'Perhaps you'd be kind enough to take me to Mr Sanders so we can sort this thing out. There's no point my discussing it with *you*.'

'There's certainly no point your discussing it with anyone else,' came the terse answer. 'I'm Jake Sanders.'

'*Jake* Sanders?' Emma gulped. 'But . . . my letter was from Jane Sanders.'

'You misread my signature. There's no Jane as I just said, and I'm a bachelor.'

Emma felt like bursting into tears. 'I'm terribly sorry Mr . . . er . . . Sanders. I—I thought—I mean, I mistook you for the chauffeur.'

'If I'd known I was meeting a fashion plate I'd have changed!' he replied with a sting, his derisive glance taking in her mascara-streaked face, limp hair and stained dress.

Flushing at his sarcasm, she sank down on one of her cases. Her legs felt like jelly and she was trembling with nerves and tiredness. What a dreadful mistake she had made! She would never have accepted a job with a bachelor—unless he was in his dotage. And this one was far from that!

'Well, you'd better get in,' he told her abruptly, and pointed to the Mercedes. 'I'll put your cases in the boot.'

She stood up, obeying like a robot, and climbed into the sports car. With a roar, they were off like a rocket, and for the first few minutes they were both silent as he drove out of the airport and on to the motorway.

'By the way, what's your name?' Jake Sanders asked as the speedometer touched a hundred.

'Emma Porter.'

'Oh God!' He banged the steering wheel with his hand. 'You're the last one I wanted!'

'In that case I'll return to England tomorrow.'

'You won't,' he said vehemently. 'I need a cook and you'll have to do. It's this ridiculous sex-discrimination act that's caused the mistake. If I'd been allowed to advertise for a male cook none of this would have happened.'

'But you said you'd engaged a man?'

'So I did; and I now realise how the mistake must have occurred. I received so many replies that I decided to make mine very brief to save time. Yours and Monsieur Roche's were the last two I had to send off. I had a phone call just as I was slipping them into the envelopes, and I must have put them in the wrong ones.' He sighed with exasperation. 'I suppose I shall have to make the best of a bad job. I won't expect much from you, naturally. If I remember correctly, you're the girl who thought enthusiasm could take the place of experience.'

She turned to look at him. His handsome face was

set and angry.

'I don't think it's fair to blame me for your mistake,' she reproached. 'If you want me to stay, I shall do my best, and I don't think you'll be disappointed. I haven't had any practical experience, but I have a natural flair, and——'

'Flair!' he exploded. 'My guests and I are used to gourmet cooking, not the fumblings of an amateur! Hell, you don't even speak Spanish, do you?'

Emma's lips trembled at his harsh words, and she was once more close to tears. The strain of the journey, the error at the airport, together with her hostile reception, was almost too much.

'Nothing was mentioned in your advertisement about speaking Spanish,' she said in a wobbly voice.

'I know.' His own voice was gruff and contained a hint of apology. 'I forgot to put it in. That's why I was so careful whom I chose. I had several other excellent offers apart from the chef I was expecting from the Dorchester, but turned them all down because they didn't speak the language. Unlike most European countries, the people here don't speak much English, and shopping could be difficult for you.'

'That's my worry. I'm sure I'll get by with sign language and a dictionary. I'm not a complete idiot, you know.'

He turned his head away from the road for a moment. 'I'll take your word for that,' he said with a hint of a smile. 'You're quite right, of course. I can hardly blame you for my own mistake. We'll just have to get by as best we can. I'm sure if you stick to basics you won't go far wrong. And at least you're no beauty, so that's one problem solved.'

Emma was speechless with indignation. Mr Sanders' condescension, and assumption that her skills were minimal, irritated her almost as much as his anger had done. But to have him tell her he was delighted that she looked a sight, and know that he assumed she always looked this way, was more than she could bear. Her know-it-all employer was going to have two lessons to learn: one, that he would not have to 'get by' with her cooking, and two, that she was an attractive young woman with an excellent figure. Yet even as she thought this, she amended it. On the question of cooking she had every intention of making him eat his words—along with the food. But as to her appearance, she was not so sure. Perhaps it might be better—and safer—for him to continue finding her unprepossessing.

He was obviously still angry with himself and, unjustly, with her. Even with his face set and grim he was devastatingly handsome. His long-fingered hands were steady on the wheel, and he handled the powerful car skilfully. The blond hairs on his arms were bleached almost white, and Emma was intensely aware of his well muscled body as his hand brushed against her thigh when he changed gear. There was an almost hypnotic aura surrounding him, so intense was his attraction.

They turned up a wide dirt track road and within a few moments entered the wrought iron gates that led to a large white stone villa, the verandah arched, and lit by lanterns. Jake Sanders drew the car to a halt outside the oak front door, and came round to help her out.

'I was going to put you—or rather the cook I was expecting—in the staff quarters over the garage, but I think you'll be happier in the main house,' he told her as he led her through the hall and up the curved wrought iron stairway with its polished brass handrail.

He opened one of the doors on the landing and she followed him into the bedroom. It was furnished simply but expensively. The rough plaster walls were stippled white, but the beams across the ceiling had been left in their original teak, while the wicker-headed bed, covered with a dazzling blue, white and black striped bedcover, matched the curtains at the window. The floor was quarry-tiled and dotted with large white fur rugs.

'There's a bathroom adjoining,' he told her, pointing to the opposite door, 'and the terrace overlooks the sea. Carmen, the maid, doesn't live in, but gets here about eight. Her English isn't good, but if you speak slowly, she'll understand. She'll show you the ropes, and if there's anything you can't find out from her, come to me.' He was about to walk out, but then hesitated in the doorway. 'Are you hungry?'

She shook her head. 'I wouldn't mind a cup of coffee, though. Perhaps I could make one for you too?'

He did not respond to her overture. 'I'll show you where the kitchen is,' he said, and turned away.

She followed him down to the gleaming modern kitchen that led off from the dining area. 'We're all electric here,' he said, and pointed to the Neff double oven and black ceramic hob. 'I hope you're used to it?'

'I can cook on either,' Emma replied with some slight satisfaction.

She filled the electric kettle that stood on the teak formica countertop, and after opening a dazzling succession of cupboard doors, found cups and saucers and the coffee.

'Not for me,' Jake Sanders told her abruptly as she took out two cups. 'Help yourself to whatever you want. I'll see you in the morning.' Turning on his heels, he went out.

Emma opened one of the doors of the huge American fridge-freezer, and found a carton of milk in the well stocked interior. Seated on a wickerwork stool at the countertop bar, she sipped the hot drink and glanced around admiringly at the fitments. The units were in a light matt oak which blended well with the beams and the red quarry-tiled floor. Above the double bowl of the stainless steel sink unit was a picture window which overlooked the garden and floodlit pool. She would have liked to have looked around the house, but decided to wait until the following morning in case Mr Sanders had not gone to bed. She was frightened that if he found her nosing about he would be annoyed. Sighing, she rinsed her cup and saucer and made her way back to her room.

By the time she had finished unpacking it was nearly two o'clock, but although she was tired she had to have a bath. Luckily the water was hot, and she soaked contentedly in the large, navy sunken tub before drying herself on a turkish towel luxurious enough for a queen.

What an eventful day this had been! Her new employer seemed cold and unfriendly, and she was not sure if she wanted to remain here. She would give it a week and see how things worked out. Perhaps when he got over his annoyance for the mistake he had made in engaging her and had tasted her cooking, he might warm towards her. It seemed an impossible hope. He was a sophisticated man used to women as attractive and worldly as himself. And from the way he had acted towards her, he had not even seen her as a woman. She was purely an irritating appendage whom he would like to have sent back on the next plane, had it been at all viable.

Emma wondered how he could afford to live in such luxury. He was not much more than thirty, yet he kept this expensive villa, with a cook and a maid. From what she had glimpsed of the house, it did not have the air of a rented holiday home, but one that was lived in and enjoyed.

Perhaps he was independently wealthy, with a rich family back in England. He might even be living here as a tax exile—or have a business on the island. It was pointless to speculate. No doubt she would find out in due course.

Padding over to the bed, she climbed between the blue sheets. Silk, she saw, and felt so sinful that she giggled. If only her grandparents could see her now! Remembering she was alone in the house with a man, she decided it was best that they couldn't.

Taking her strange reception into account—combined with finding out that she would not be working for a family as she had assumed, but for a bad-tempered bachelor—she still did not regret her decision to come here. If Jake Sanders proved impossible to please, it should not be difficult in the holiday season to find another job on the island. Certainly nothing would induce her to return to England. She would stay until September, come what may.

CHAPTER TWO

EMMA was awoken at seven the following morning by her alarm, and she stretched lazily, reluctant to get up after her short night's rest. She relaxed for a further five minutes, then crossed over the room and opened the sliding doors that led on to her balcony.

The view that met her gaze was spectacular. The villa was situated on a modest incline. Shrubs and bushes flowered in a profusion of green, gold and red, and pine and eucalyptus trees led down to the bay, where the amethyst blue sea lapped lazily on to the golden sands of the beach.

The air was perfectly still, except for the sweet notes of the birds. No traffic disturbed the tranquillity. Indeed, there was no road between the villa and the bay. Nor could Emma see other houses either to the left or the right. They appeared to be completely isolated.

The garden, with its circular pool and perfectly manicured green spiky grass, lay dewily perfect in the morning light. The sky was bright blue, and the slight haze on the horizon gave an inkling of the heat to come. Even now it must have been about seventy, for though she only wore the flimsiest cotton nightdress, she still felt warm.

Taking a final breath of the sweet-scented air, she returned to her room to dress. Remembering her intention to look dowdy, she put her contact lenses back in their little box and put on her glasses, then scraped her hair back from her face and pinned it there with several large, unsightly-looking clips which she normally used when setting her hair. A careful application of dark eyeshadow under her lids gave her a weary air, as did the heavily applied eyebrow pencil, with which she deliberately gave herself downward curving brows. Grinning impishly at her unsightly face, she went to the wardrobe. Only then did she pause. Normally she did her shopping with her grandmother, but the last time, urged on by the feeling that it was now or never, she had gone alone and used all her carefully hoarded allowance to buy herself a young, pretty wardrobe suitable for a working holiday in the sun. Regretfully she pushed her newest clothes into the back, and drew forward a few old dresses she had planned to wear in the kitchen. Yet even these were too attractive, and she took out a blue shirred sundress and carefully snipped the elastic. The shirring disappeared and she was left with a blue sack, which she donned, giggling at the thought of Jake Sanders' face when he saw her.

Silently she went downstairs. No one was about, and she took advantage of the hour to look around.

In the daylight the villa appeared even larger than she

had assumed. The main rooms overlooked the pool and the bay beyond, and a wide terrace afforded shade, with vines growing around graceful white pillars. It was comfortably furnished with blue wicker chairs and couches scattered with white linen cushions.

The pool was tiled in blue and green mosaic and white wood furniture bordered it, while in one corner stood a white trellis pagoda, containing a well stocked bar, indicating that the inner—as well as the outer man's comfort—was well tended to.

The water looked so tempting that she longed to have a swim, and made up her mind to ask her employer if she would be allowed to do so in the early morning. Regretfully she turned back to the house and the main living room, where the leather settees and armchairs were in the same shades of caramel and browns as the long-haired rugs which were scattered on the tiled floor. The outside of the house might be typically Spanish in appearance, but the interior was strictly twentieth-century Heals.

Several startlingly modern paintings hung on the walls, among which she spotted a Hockney and a Warhol. She was staring admiringly at one of the African bronze masks that dotted the room, when she heard a woman's voice.

'Good morning, *señorita.*'

Emma turned to see a short, plump, dark-haired woman of about fifty, standing with a shopping basket over one arm.

'You must be Carmen,' she said.

The woman nodded and smiled. 'And you . . .?'

'I'm Emma Porter, the new cook.'

The woman looked at her with astonishment. '*You* cook? Me expect man. Mr Sanders he say no woman cook this time.'

'There was a mistake. Mr Sanders was also expecting a

man,' Emma explained slowly, and went on to tell Carmen what had happened the previous evening. 'But why didn't Mr Sanders want a woman?' she finally asked as she ended her tale.

Carmen chuckled, but refused to be drawn. 'You ask Mr Sanders. He tell.'

Emma followed her into the kitchen and made herself breakfast of toast and coffee. The sliced bread was of the same rubbery substance as in England, she noted, and while hunting for marmalade as the maid unpacked her shopping basket, she found that all the labels on the jars and packages were familiar, right down to the Fairy Liquid!

'Does Mr Sanders have breakfast in his room?' she asked.

'No, he like on terrace. Always he swim early, then eat at nine. Fresh orange juice, coffee, two piece toast—no crust—and marmalade. Today I show you.'

For the next half hour Carmen explained where everything was kept and how all the gadgets worked. Emma found a pad and pencil and noted it all down, knowing it would be impossible to remember otherwise. Apart from the electric hob there was a Calor gas one that was only used in emergencies, and from the amount of power cuts they appeared to get, this could be quite often. Sometimes they might not have any for weeks, and then two or three in succession. It was going to be difficult to plan menus with this haphazard system, and she hoped her employer did not give too many dinner parties that relied on complicated dishes being finished off at the last moment in the oven. Still, if the rest of the island could manage, so could she.

Promptly at eight-thirty she saw the broad-shouldered figure of Jake Sanders through the kitchen window as he made his way to the pool. There was not an ounce of superfluous flesh on him, and she could not contain a thrill of pleasure as she watched his expert dive from the board into the blue water. After several leisurely lengths, he emerged some twenty minutes later and shook his blond head like a puppy to free the globules that clung to him. He disappeared from view as he made his way back in to change, and as she turned back to watch Carmen setting his tray, the older woman shook her head and laughed.

'He good-looking, yes?'

Emma blushed and nodded. 'Is Mr Sanders engaged?'

The maid shrugged. 'I no sure. His lady come here to stay soon.'

Her voice was so unenthusiastic that it was obvious she did not approve of her employer's girl-friend, but Emma did not question her further, feeling it was wrong to pry too much.

It was just on nine when Emma took the tray from Carmen and carried it out to the patio. Jake Sanders was already seated, dressed in white shorts and a navy cotton T-shirt, with his feet bare.

'Sleep well?' he greeted her.

'Very,' she lied. 'It's so quiet here. I'm used to peaceful surroundings myself, but we do occasionally hear the noise of an aeroplane or car!'

'That's why I chose to build here. We're out of the flight path to the airport, and the main road's some distance away. You do drive, don't you?'

'Yes,' she replied, glad she was able to answer one of his requirements.

'Thank heavens for that. I wouldn't want to have to chauffeur you around shopping, and Carmen doesn't drive. How did you get on with her?'

'Very well. Her English is better than I expected, and she's been very patient showing me the ropes.'

'She's a good sort. I've had her for three years, ever since I built the house. Her husband does the garden and her daughters act as waitresses if I have a party and need extra help.' A smile quirked his lips. 'We're one big happy family, and I hope you'll become part of it.'

Warmed by his sudden change of tone, Emma asked him if it would be all right if she used the pool.

'Whenever you like,' he answered airily. 'Until my visitors arrive there won't be a great deal for you to do. When I'm here on my own I don't entertain much, so if I were you I'd take advantage of the next few weeks. After that you'll be kept busy.'

'How many guests are you expecting?'

He did not answer at once, but motioned her to sit down opposite him. 'How about a cup of coffee?' he asked.

She accepted his offer, and sipped it while he munched at his toast.

'This is just how I like it,' he said appreciatively as he finished the second piece. 'You've made a good start.'

'If you think my toast is good, wait till you've tasted my boiled eggs!' Emma retorted, incensed that he was treating her like an imbecilic child again. How far wrong could one go making a piece of toast? Not that she had even made it, but there was no point saying so.

'I suppose I deserved that,' he replied. His periwinkle blue eyes glinted and became even more startling in colour. 'But there's no need to frown at me.'

'I'm not frowning.'

'Your eyebrows are.' He stared at her. 'Do you always pencil them in like that?'

'Yes, I think it suits me. Don't you?'

He almost choked on his coffee, but manfully said nothing.

'You still haven't told me how many guests you're expecting,' she said, keeping her face straight.

'So I didn't. Well, there's my brother and his wife, with their year-old baby, and the nanny. They'll be here in a couple of weeks, and are staying until the beginning of September. My brother will probably be returning to England on business for the odd day or two, but he'll be here most of the time. Celia—a friend of mine—is also coming, and she'll probably stay even longer. I'm not sure of her plans yet.' He paused, waiting for her comment. 'Cat got your tongue, Miss Porter?' he asked after a few moments.

'I'm sorry, Mr Sanders, I wasn't sure if you'd finished.'

'Yes, I have. I hope you'll be able to cater for everyone? If not, I'd rather you told me now.'

'I'm sure I can manage. After all, I was expecting to cater for a *family* when I accepted the job.'

'How fortunate for you that you're getting one to practise on! I only hope your confidence in your ability is well founded.'

'I'll try not to give you cause for complaint,' she answered stiffly. 'Is there anything special you'd like me to prepare for you today?'

'I'll leave the menus up to you. I don't want two big meals a day, though. A snack lunch is fine. You'll find the freezer well stocked, and I think Carmen brought in fruit and vegetables with her today.'

Emma stood up. 'Do you want me to wear a uniform? I've brought several white aprons with me.'

'Keep them for the kitchen. We're very informal here.' He looked at her unshapely cotton dress with open criticism. 'You can even wear jeans if you prefer. I assume you do *have* a body between the folds of that thing?'

'I'm more comfortable in a loose dress when I'm working,' she replied demurely.

'You arrived wearing a loose dress too,' he said. 'You're

obviously fond of them, Miss Porter.'

'Please call me Emma,' she said, hoping to establish a more cordial atmosphere between them. Though he had said he wanted a plain-looking female as a cook, he had made no mention of treating her like a servant. Yet he merely nodded at her suggestion, and did not ask her to call him Jake. Informality did not appear to stretch *that* far!

Still, maybe it was better to keep her distance. Peter would definitely think so. At the thought of him she felt uncomfortable. What would he say when he found she was living on her own with a man? A chair scraped behind her and she turned and saw that Jake Sanders had risen.

'I'm going to be out for the rest of the day, but I shall be back for dinner. Don't attempt anything too elaborate. Rather wholesome than loathsome!' he concluded.

'Yes, sir,' Emma answered. 'I'll take great care not to burn the ice cream!'

She picked up the tray and marched off to the kitchen. What an infuriating man he was! Friendly and encouraging one minute, and rude the next. Well, she would show him a thing or two tonight!

Carmen disappeared to clean the bedrooms and Emma opened the refrigerator and then the freezer to examine the contents. Jake Sanders had not exaggerated when he had told her they were well stocked. The meat trays contained an assortment of lamb, beef, veal and poultry, all neatly labelled with the weights and portions. There were packets of prawns, scampi and smoked salmon, as well as several large cartons of fresh whipped cream. She learned from the maid that this was specially imported frozen because the cream on the island was always slightly sour, and that Mr Sanders was very partial to rich desserts.

The array of cheese was equally dazzling. Camembert, Brie, Boursin, Bel Paese, Stilton, Cheddar—the world's best. It appeared her employer was partial to cheese as well!

She went to her room and brought down the half a dozen cookery books she had brought with her, and tried to compose a balanced menu for this evening's meal. Before making a final choice, she questioned Carmen over lunch.

'Is there anything Mr Sanders positively dislikes?'

The maid's homely face frowned as she tried to think. 'He very easy, but very fussy. You cook good, he like. Cook bad, he angry.' She waved her plump arms about as she explained. 'Last cook like use lots pepper. Mr Sanders no like, but she still use. One day she made soup, full black pepper. Mr Sanders he come kitchen and pour down sink, then tell her pack bags and go.'

Emma's normally firm hand trembled as she noted down some recipes and their page number. Fancy throwing the woman out—and probably with nowhere to go. He certainly sounded ruthless when crossed.

She busily set to, defrosting the scampi in the sun and peeling the leeks and potatoes for vichyssoise. The cream was slightly sweetened, but not enough to notice once it was mixed in with the soup. There were chicken stock cubes in the cupboard, and within an hour she had the first course prepared.

She was about to start skinning the tomatoes for the Provençal sauce, when the telephone rang. She hesitated before answering it, but as Carmen made no move towards it, she finally took the call.

It was Jake Sanders.

'Miss Porter . . . Emma? I'm bringing two business friends back with me for dinner. They're only here for the day and I want them to have a typically Spanish meal. See what you can rustle up. We'll be home at seven-thirty.'

Before she could protest that she had already prepared dinner, he rang off.

Emma set to work again, viciously chopping an onion as if it was Jake Sanders' head. What an inconsiderate man he was! He knew she had no experience of Spanish cooking, yet on her first day here he expected her to rustle up an Iberian menu fit for guests. Why couldn't he have taken them out to eat instead of expecting her to miraculously produce a meal in a few hours? Unless he had done it on purpose. Of course, that was it. No doubt he was irritated because she appeared confident that she could please him, and this was his way of putting her in her place. Well, she would show him exactly where her place was: top of her year at the Cordon Bleu.

By the early afternoon Emma had prepared most of the meal. First she would make a Spanish omelette; not very original, but the best she could do in the time. As a main course there would be scampi paella, and for dessert she had found *flan de naranjas* among her cookery cards. It was only a dressed up orange egg custard, but it was apparently a traditional dish, and looked extremely good when made in a contrasting green dish.

Carmen was a great help, and bustled round clearing up after her. She clucked admiringly as she tasted the orange custard with its topping of powdered cinnamon, and then showed Emma how her employer liked the table set on the patio. Apparently meals were never eaten inside in the summer, and even in the winter months it was often warm enough to dine al fresco.

Carmen left at six, telling Emma that her youngest daughter, Maria, would be there at eight to help serve and then wash up.

With relief Emma surveyed the meal. Even the salad was prepared in a large wooden bowl, and the Paella only needed finishing in a moderate oven for forty minutes. There had not been enough time to make individual hors d'oeuvres, so she had contented herself with whipping up cheese sticks, which only needed heating for a couple of minutes at the last moment.

Feeling reasonably satisfied with her afternoon's work, she decided to have a quick swim to refresh herself. Even now it was very warm outside, though the interior of the house never got the sun, and was as cool as if it were air-conditioned.

The water in the pool was like a warm bath, and she dived in expertly from the board, leisurely crawling up and down for a quarter of an hour. Emma swam well and enjoyed it, having been good enough to represent her school. She regretted that there was no pool near Oakton, and she had therefore been unable to keep up her standard. It also meant she had not bought a costume since leaving school. The ill-fitting black one-piece suit did nothing to enhance her figure, but she had brought it along, fully intending to buy some pretty bikinis on her first day off. Now it looked as if her old one would have to do. At least it fitted her dowdy image.

Afterwards she washed her hair and blew it dry, then twisted it into a hard bun, which made her look efficient. Then down to the kitchen again to switch on the oven. To her horror she found that the dial was stuck on 288 degrees. No matter how hard she tried, she could not get it to budge. She would have to give the paella at least an hour and a half to make up for the low temperature. But she refused to panic. It was only seven-thirty, and the main course would not be needed until nine at the earliest.

When Jake Sanders came into the kitchen, she had just taken the cheese straws from the oven, and Carmen's young daughter Maria, who had arrived on the dot of eight, was arranging them on a silver tray.

Her employer had already changed for the evening and was immaculate in blue slacks and navy silk sweater, his thick blond hair sleek as sealskin.

'Manage all right?' he enquired.

'Yes, thank you. Though it was rather a rush. I hope the menu meets with your approval, Mr Sanders. Perhaps you'd like to know what I'm going to serve.'

'I'd rather you surprised me. It will give me some idea of what I can expect if I leave the choice up to you. Incidentally, can we eat sharp at nine? My friends have to catch the one o'clock flight to London and I'm running them to the airport.' He took a cheese straw from the tray and ate it, then took another. 'These are delicious.'

'Thank you.'

'Let's hope the dinner turns out as well,' he added.

Emma held on to her temper. He was trying to rile her and she was determined not to let him.

'Carmen tells me you like to choose the wines,' she said, 'but as you weren't here, I decided on Chablis with the paella.' She showed him the bottle she had picked out. Part of her course had been devoted to wines, and she had admired and appreciated his excellent cellar.

'So you did learn *something* in your little backwater?' He appeared surprised. 'Put it in the fridge. I like it served very cold.'

'Even in Oakton we know how to serve wine,' she replied, unable to resist rebuking him for his condescending manner.

He looked unchastened and was about to leave the kitchen when she stopped him.

'By the way, there's something wrong with the oven. The thermostat appears to be stuck.'

He looked alarmed. 'Haven't you been able to use it?'

'Oh yes. But it won't get hot enough.'

'Tell Carmen about it in the morning,' he replied with

slight irritation, as if this minor domestic upset was no concern of his. 'She'll get an electrician down.'

As soon as he left Emma placed the paella in the oven and Maria disappeared on to the patio with the cheese straws. At eight-forty she prepared the omelette and then went out to the terrace to announce that dinner was ready. Jake Sanders—for some reason Emma could not think of him as Mr Sanders—was seated on a hammock deep in conversation with one of his guests, a portly, balding man of about fifty with an American accent. His companion was of a similar stocky build, but had a thin moustache and wore glasses. They were both smoking outsize cigars and she noticed they did not remove them from their mouths even when they were talking.

She stood hesitantly in the doorway for a moment, embarrassed at having to interrupt them.

Her employer spotted her and looked up. 'Yes?'

'Dinner is ready, if you'd like to sit down,' she said shyly.

They stood up and, from the way they hurriedly seated themselves, she had the impression they were hungry. It was fortunate she had made such a man-sized meal.

The plates were heating in the warmer and she placed a large portion of the omelette on each one. The remainder she popped back in the small oven, telling Maria to wait and see if further helpings would be needed.

While she disappeared with the laden trolley, Emma took the opportunity of wandering in the garden for five minutes to cool off. The pool was floodlit and the mosaic tiled fish at the bottom looked almost real. She slipped off her sandals and seated herself at the edge, allowing her feet to dangle in the still warm water. The air was soft and balmy, with just a hint of a breeze blowing in from the sea a few hundred yards away through the pinewoods.

She could hear the faint hum of conversation coming

from the diners, and it reminded her to make her way back to the house. As she neared the kitchen Maria came running out and almost banged into her.

'Señorita Emma! Come quick. *Inciendio, inciendio!*'

Emma knew very little Spanish, but the smoke billowing from the oven out into the garden made translation unnecessary. She rushed to open the oven door and the heat almost knocked her back. It was sufficient to glue her mascarad eyelashes together, and momentarily she was unable to focus.

She spluttered and coughed, and her smoke-filled eyes ran with tears as another black cloud billowed out from the flaming paella. Hurriedly she looked about for something to extinguish the fire, and grabbing the siphon of soda standing next to her on the formica top, which Maria had fortuitously forgotten to put away, she pressed down the nozzle.

'What the hell is going on?'

Startled by the thunderous voice, Emma whirled around, her hand still on the nozzle. The sight of Jake Sanders' elegant figure froze her fingers to the siphon, and a jet of soda water sprayed him with full force.

Drink in hand, he stood there, dripping water from his blond hair down to his once immaculate slacks.

'If it's all the same to you, Emma,' he said in a very quiet voice, 'I have sufficient soda in my whisky now!'

Horrified, she went on staring at him. Then shock gave her the giggles. She tried to speak, but found it impossible.

'I assume your effervescent mood has nothing to do with your culinary achievements,' he said witheringly, looking at the charred dish.

Emma's hysteria went as quickly as it had come; replaced by tears that threatened to fall.

'I don't understand,' she gulped. 'The oven was terribly

low. How *could* it have burned?'

'It obviously *wasn't* on low, or this wouldn't have happened,' he answered scathingly, as he attempted to dry himself with his handkerchief. Then he turned to look at the temperature gauge on the front panel. 'I thought you told me this wasn't working properly?'

'It isn't. The thermostat won't go above 288. That's almost cool enough to cook meringues,' she pointed out defensively.

'Not in Centigrade it isn't,' he flared. 'Didn't you know Continental settings aren't in Fahrenheit?'

Aghast, she stared at him. Why on earth hadn't such an obvious thing occurred to her? 'I never thought,' she whispered.

'That much I've gathered! But if you want to stay here, I suggest you start.' He strode to the door. 'If you've got some more of that omelette, we'll have it with bread. We're all still ravenous!'

Fortunately the remainder of the omelette was not affected by the smoke from the main oven, although it was no longer creamy inside. Still, it would have to do. Emma set about heating up some French bread and while that was crisping, she pushed the blackened remains of the paella into the waste disposal.

What a disastrous start! No doubt Jake Sanders was congratulating himself that his first assessment of her had been correct, and was regaling his guests with the amusing tale.

Perhaps after tonight he might even try to find someone else. Wearily she sat down at the kitchen table and sipped at her black coffee. She had no appetite for supper. She could still taste the smoke at the back of her throat and it felt more and more irritated, to match her mood.

When Maria returned with the empty dessert dish she hoped that Jake Sanders might have sent a consoling message back with her. But the young girl said nothing, merely setting to and washing the silver cutlery and Waterford glasses with a good-humoured smile on her face.

'Why you no go bed?' she said. 'I clear away everything.'

'No, I'll wait until they've finished. Mr Sanders might want to speak to me before he goes out again.'

Emma waited up until she heard the front door slam soon after eleven, and then made her way to her room. Before she left, Maria had put everything away, and even washed the kitchen floor, so there was nothing left to do downstairs. Carmen would clear the dining table in the morning and no doubt make another attempt at cleaning the burnt paella dish, which had obstinately remained charred for all Maria's furious scrubbing.

Emma stood on her balcony, gazing out at the moonlit sea, its bright light reflecting in silver ripples on the water. Each star twinkled luminously in the clear sky, and as the noise of the cicadas increased in intensity, and then fell back to a quiet hum, she sighed contentedly. Even though her boss was rude and difficult, this setting made it worth while sticking it out.

Besides, she was not going to give Peter and her grandparents the opportunity of being proved right. She knew that in some ways she was young for her years, but she was not a fool—despite what Jake Sanders thought.

Fortunately he had not noticed her tears this evening, or if he had, he had put it down to the smoke. She certainly did not want him to realise how much she wanted to stay here. She had to appear independent. He would never respect her otherwise. But why should she want his respect? She did not know the answer. All she knew was that she wanted it.

She walked into the bathroom and undressed in front

of the long mirror, inspecting herself critically as she did so. Her breasts were high and firm, and her small waist and shapely legs could withstand any competition. She might be tiny, but she was perfectly proportioned. She reddened. What had precipitated this sudden interest in her body? She did not have to search too hard for the answer. It was Jake Sanders.

Yet how could she be attracted to a man she hardly knew, and who was barely aware of her existence? But then she had never met a man like him before. Compared with Peter, he was. . . . Refusing to finish the thought, she undid her hair from its hard little bun, and let the thick dark brown tresses flow loosely over her shoulders. It was certainly an improvement, and far more flattering to her heart-shaped face. She peered at her lashes, which were thick and long, but hardly enhanced by the light touch of mascara she used, then ran her fingers lightly over her face. Her olive skin held no blemishes and she tanned easily and quickly. Emma smiled at her reflection. No matter how used he was to lovely women, if Jake Sanders saw her now, he would undoubtedly give her a second look.

Slipping on her nightgown, she climbed into bed. Although she was alone in a strange house in a strange country, she did not feel nervous. Somehow Majorca was bewitching her. Its peacefulness and calm beauty were eliciting a feeling of well-being and contentedness. It was as if she had been cast away on this island for years, instead of hours. Nothing mattered in the outside world, because here, in this remote spot she was cocooned from it.

If her dreams were so much sweeter, who was to say that they might *not* become reality?

CHAPTER THREE

Emma was down before Carmen arrived, feeling refreshed after a good night's sleep. She swam for a while before making her way to the kitchen to fix herself a large breakfast. She only realised why she was feeling particularly hungry when she remembered she had not eaten anything the previous evening. What a fiasco her first dinner had been! Later she might be able to laugh at it. But for the moment the memory was still too raw.

Heaping her toast with strawberry jam, she ate outside, while Carmen clucked angrily at the sticky frying pan, as she tried to clean it. Finally she came outside to Emma.

'No more you cook Spanish,' she instructed with a smile. 'Mr Sanders he like French very much. Is fond steak with wine sauce.'

'Thanks.' Emma was grateful to know this, since she wanted to cook something he really liked to make up for last night. 'I'll take a steak out right away.'

The steaks, rump and entrecôte, were in neat piles in the freezer, each one clearly labelled, and she decided on a tournedos which, with the addition of the liver pâté she found in the same compartment, would make a base for a Tournedos Rossini.

While Carmen waddled off to do the rest of the housework, Emma prepared a Niçoise salad for lunch. Perhaps tomorrow she would ask Carmen to take her into Paguera and show her the shops, then she could plan a week's menus by purchasing all the food herself. It was rather disconcerting to build up meals around Carmen's daily choice of vegetables. But she did not fancy the prospect of driving the Mercedes, whose dashboard looked confusingly like a computer when compared with her functional Mini. But it would be impossible to carry much shopping in this heat and she had no option but to use the car. But first she would explore the nearby territory, and this afternoon would go to the beach.

'Good morning, Emma.' Jake Sanders' cool voice interrupted her reverie and she looked up to see him by the doorway.

'I'll have bacon and eggs this morning, please.' His instructions were crisp. 'I hope you're capable of cooking the bacon without burning it?'

'I'll do my best, sir,' she answered quietly, not allowing his reminder to spoil her good humour. As if she needed reminding!

He strode out, and she set to. Within minutes four crisp pieces of bacon and two perfectly fried eggs were set before him, and before he had a chance to make any more sarcastic comments, she returned to the kitchen.

The morning flew by, and by lunchtime the Salade Niçoise was arranged in a wooden bowl ready to be served by Carmen. There was also a selection of cheese on a leaf-strewn platter, and a bowl of fresh fruit resting on a nest of ice.

'You make food look pretty,' Carmen praised her. 'Mr Sanders he like.'

'What does Mr Sanders like?' his voice demanded as he padded into the kitchen clad in a beachrobe.

'Things they look nice,' Carmen replied.

'One shouldn't judge a book by its cover,' was his sour rejoinder.

Carmen smiled. 'I bring lunch out now.'

'Let me choose my wine first.'

'I've already done so,' Emma interjected. 'I did a course on wine during my training.'

'What training?' he asked bleakly. 'I'll have some Hock.'

'That's exactly what I have chilling in the refrigerator!'

Silently he stalked out, and Emma glared at his departing back. Couldn't he forgive and forget, or did he plan to remind her of last night for the next three months? Furiously she banged down the saucepan with the Rossini sauce, and some of it splashed on to her dress. Oh well, it served her right for allowing him to get under her skin. Now she would have to change before she went down to the beach.

'I'm going for a swim in the sea,' Emma told Carmen. 'But I'll be back to prepare the tea.'

'Is very hot outside. Be careful. You not use.'

'I never burn,' Emma replied airily. 'We sometimes have sunshine in England, you know!'

Upstairs in her room, she stared at her clothes. All her remaining dresses were too pretty for her to risk wearing them, and she was obliged to pick on the loose smock dress in which she had arrived. Thank heavens she had washed and ironed it yesterday.

Packing her bag with a towel and sun-cream, and donning her one and only swimsuit—she really must go into town to buy something more becoming—she made her way through the garden to the pinewoods. The pool area was deserted, though she saw some letters lying on one of the tables, held in place by a glass paperweight. They reminded her that she had not yet asked Carmen what business Jake Sanders was in. Her mind had been too occupied to think of it.

The walk through the cool shaded woods took about five minutes. The sun dappled the dry earth as it broke through the branches, and the fresh smell of pine lingered long after she had left the trees behind. The small, almost white sandy beach was deserted, and she was surprised, until she saw a notice with *Vedado* written on it, and underneath in English, Private. This beach must belong to the villa.

Her feet were almost burned by the heat of the sand, and she hopped on one leg as she put her sandals back on again to walk down to the water's edge. The waves lapped gently on to the shore, and the water was crystal clear, with tiny fish swimming beneath.

Emma peeled off her dress and plunged into the warm sea, swimming out to the raft moored a couple of hundred yards from the shore.

She clambered on and lay there with her face to the sun, eyes closed against its glare, and the motion of the raft, as it tipped back and forth with the waves soon lulled her to sleep.

When she awoke she felt heavy-eyed. The sun was molten white in a sky washed pale by its heat, and she chided herself for foolishly falling asleep. Now she would have to keep in the shade or she would look like a boiled lobster.

She dived into the sea and swam lazily towards the shore, then floated on her back, enjoying the lilting movement of the waves as they gently washed her right on to the beach.

Glancing at her watch, she saw it was time to return to the villa, and bent to pick up her dress. As she struggled into it, she felt momentarily giddy, but she drew several deep breaths and slowly made her way up the beach towards the narrow path that eventually led on to an unmade slip road. Her dress, for all its looseness, felt tight against her skin as she walked for what seemed like hours. The terrain on either side of the lonely road was uninteresting. It was covered only by spiky bushes and odd clumps of stiff green grass in dry, dusty earth, and offered no protection against the intense heat, which hardly differed from the early afternoon.

Her legs became leaden and she was forced to sit down. She pushed her sunglasses farther up her perspiring nose, but they seemed ineffective against the glare, and when she closed her lids to rest her burning eyes, flashes of white appeared. She finally forced herself to stand and felt as if she were being whirled around like a spinning top. The bushes danced up and down, and she blinked again and again as she tried to focus. But to no avail.

Tentatively she walked on. Each step felt as if she were climbing a steep slope, although the road was perfectly flat. Her body was burning and yet she felt cold and started to shiver. When her teeth chattered uncontrollably, she panicked.

Supposing she was unable to reach the main road? She might lie here for days, and no one would think of looking for her in this quiet, uninhabited spot. She had to reach civilisation . . . had to find a house . . . call for help. . . . She stumbled on, finally reaching a junction, and thankfully heard the sound of a car coming up the dusty track.

There was a squeal of tyres as it braked suddenly, and Emma breathed a sigh of relief.

'Help me, please help me,' she heard a tiny voice squeaking, and realised it was her own.

She barely saw the man who came towards her, but his strong arms were firm around her shoulders as he guided her slowly towards his car. She felt the gentle brush of hair against her arm as he lifted her on to the front seat, but it was only as they roared off that she managed to turn her spinning head and through half-closed lids see the bearded figure of her employer.

Emma did not remember anything more, and when she finally awoke it was to find herself in her own room, with the sky outside peppered by stars. Quickly she sat up. A pain shot through her head and she gasped.

'Don't move if you can help it,' Jake Sanders said, and turning her head carefully, she saw him get up from a chair on the balcony. 'You've been a very sick girl.'

'What's wrong with me? What have I caught?' she croaked, her voice full of alarm, her memory blank.

'Nothing, except too much sun,' he answered reassuringly. 'Not content with burning the food, you thought you'd do the same thing to yourself!' He gave a short laugh. 'You did almost as good a job on it. You've got third degree burns.'

'But how . . . I don't understand. . . .'

'Because you're an obstinate child,' he retorted. 'Carmen told me she warned you, but you seemed to think the sun here was the same as in England. You've a lot to learn.'

'I'm sorry,' she said huskily. 'I've been nothing but a nuisance since I arrived. If you'd like me to leave. . . .'

'Not for the moment,' he said gravely. 'You're too ill. Anyway, I think you've learned your lesson and you may start to improve from now on. You could hardly get worse.'

Tears filled Emma's eyes. She knew he was teasing her, but also knew there was some element of truth in his words.

'Do you think I could have some water?' she asked weakly. 'My throat's dry as a bone.'

He poured her some from the carafe at the side of the bed, and placed his arm around her shoulder to help her sit up to drink it. As she did, she noticed she was wearing her nightdress.

'Did . . . did . . . Carmen undress me?'

'No, I did. Carmen left early yesterday, and I didn't fancy waiting for the doctor to arrive. You looked so hot and constricted that I thought you'd expire on me.'

Emma coloured furiously and avoided his eyes. 'I'm

sure I could have managed to undress myself if you'd woken me.'

'You weren't asleep,' he said dryly. 'You were unconscious. But don't worry. You've got nothing I haven't seen many times before!'

'I'm sure. But I still——'

'Don't make an issue of it,' he cut in wearily. 'I never rape unconscious women! Now I suggest you go to sleep again. You'll feel better when you wake up.'

'I'm not tired.'

'Close your eyes and count to sixty. But tell me when you get to forty-five.'

Obediently she did as he ordered, counting slowly, and when she opened her eyes the sun was streaming into her room, and Carmen was bending anxiously over her.

'You feel better?' the woman asked, and looked relieved as Emma nodded and lifted her head from the pillow.

For the first time she noticed the metal frame over her body, with the sheet draped over it. She gave it only a passing thought, because for the moment she was delighted to find she did not have the same blinding headache as the previous day. At least she assumed it was the previous day.

'Is it Thursday?' she asked.

Carmen nodded. 'You like something eat? Doctor he say dry toast, but if you want more . . .?'

'Tea and toast will be fine. I'm sorry to be so much trouble,' Emma replied apologetically. 'How has Mr Sanders managed about the cooking? Perhaps I can get up later and make dinner?'

'You no get up,' Carmen stated firmly. 'Doctor say you rest till Saturday. I tell you 'bout sun, but you very bad . . . foolish.'

'I know,' Emma agreed, smiling faintly. 'But I'm sure I can manage to cook Mr Sanders a meal.'

'He eat food I cook or go out eat. You no worry 'bout him.'

While Carmen waddled off to make breakfast, Emma thought over the last few days. It was a wonder Mr Sanders hadn't fired her. Or was he waiting until she was better before doing it? She had given him sufficient reason, having behaved stupidly over the electric oven and childishly over sunburning herself.

Well, at least he had seen that her body was not that of a child! The realisation made her gasp. She might have made her face and hair look as unprepossessing as possible, but physically. . . . She blushed, horrified by her erotic imaginings. What on earth had come over her?

There was a soft tap at the door, and at her response, the man on her mind stepped into the room: tall, tanned and far too handsome for any girl's peace of mind.

'And how are you today?' he asked cheerfully. 'Carmen tells me you're hungry, so that's a good sign.'

'I thought I'd get up.'

'Not until Dr Marcos has seen you. He'll be along this morning.'

Carmen brought the tray in and set it down in front of Emma, who eagerly picked up the toast. But after a few bites she felt nauseous and lay back on her pillow.

'I think I'll just have the tea,' she said faintly.

'Not getting up yet?' her employer asked, straight-faced.

'Never!'

He chuckled, though sympathetically. 'You'll feel much better tomorrow. But meanwhile I've got some pills here for you. They'll help your nausea.'

He filled a glass of water and handed her a pill, which she just managed to swallow.

'Why have I got this frame over me?' she asked.

'Because every time the sheet touched your body, you

moaned. If I hadn't managed to get the doctor immediately, you might well have been hospitalised.'

'It's incredible! I only sat out for a few hours.'

'My dear girl, you're in the Mediterranean, not Margate. Haven't you ever holidayed abroad?'

'No. My parents were killed when I was young, and my grandparents dislike travelling. Other than school trips, I've not been out of England.'

He looked astonished. 'How old did you say you were?'

'Twenty-one.'

'Surely you're old enough to go off on holidays on your own—or with your boy-friend? You do have one, I assume?'

She nodded. 'Yes. But we wouldn't go away together. Neither of us approve of the honeymoon before the wedding!'

His lips curved into a smile at her comment. 'So you're engaged?'

'Not yet. That's why I wanted to get away from home for a while. My grandparents would like me to marry Peter, but I'm not certain how I feel about him.'

'If you're so indecisive, you don't love him.'

'Are you an authority on love?'

'The best you're likely to meet,' he said solemnly. 'The minute I get the symptoms, I dose myself with medicine.'

Emma was amused. The pill was working and she felt better able to cope with her employer's sense of humour. 'What's the antidote to love?'

'Travel. A long journey, as far away as possible from the object of one's desire.'

'Women aren't objects,' she said forcefully.

'They are to me!'

'What brought you out to Majorca?' she asked boldly, taking advantage of his mellow mood to learn something about him.

'The same reason as you—to get away from my family.' She waited for him to elaborate, and he caught her curious gaze. 'I'm the black sheep,' he confided with a grin. 'And I love it!'

Emma smiled, not sure whether to take him seriously. 'Don't you see your parents?'

'Not if I can help it.'

'Don't you ever go home?'

'I'm at home now.'

'I'm sorry,' Emma said gently.

'You don't need to be.' He shrugged his powerful shoulders. 'I'm fond of my parents, but we don't get on. They disapprove of the way I earn my living. The Brewery is their lives, and I sometimes think that if my father cut himself, pale ale would run out!'

'What part of the country do you come from?' she asked.

'Somerset. My family have lived in Banyon Manor for generations—and no doubt my brother will carry on the tradition.'

'Do you get on with him?'

'Yes—although we're very different. He and his wife are a great couple. In fact she was my first love.' He stopped abruptly and lapsed into silence.

'What happened?' she prodded.

'She had too much sense to marry me. Which was a good thing for both of us—I'd have made a lousy husband. But you'll like Pam. She's very easy-going.'

'Didn't you say they're bringing a nanny with them?'

He nodded. 'She was mine when I was a child.'

Emma was disappointed. She had been hoping for the company of another young girl.

'She'll probably want to prepare the baby's food herself,' he continued. 'Watch the way she does coddled eggs and steamed fish. You might learn a thing or two!'

'You're never going to let me forget that dinner, are you?'

'It's up to you to make me. If. . . .' He broke off as he heard the front door chime. 'That must be the doctor,' he said, and discreetly left the room as Dr Marcos entered.

His examination was quick but thorough, and he advised Emma to stay out of the sun until her skin had completely peeled.

'Mr Sanders wanted to get you a nurse,' he informed her, 'but I told him it wasn't necessary. However, he sat up with you the first night himself.'

Emma was surprised at Jake Sanders' concern for her, but knew it was foolish to read anything significant into it. All it showed was that beneath his teasing exterior, he was a kind man.

When Dr Marcos left she immediately fell asleep, and awoke later in the evening, feeling much better. She attacked her boiled eggs with gusto, and managed to finish the two slices of buttered toast which Carmen prepared for her.

The woman looked approvingly at the empty tray when she came up to collect it. 'Tomorrow you much better.'

'I'm better now,' Emma smiled. 'Is Mr Sanders going out for dinner?'

'Yes, but he back by ten. He say to tell you.'

'Do you think you could find me something to read before you leave? I don't feel tired, and I didn't bring any books with me.'

A few minutes later Carmen reappeared with a thick tome. 'This make you keep awake. Very sexy!' She beamed mischievously. 'I see you in morning.'

Emma turned her attention to the lurid cover. A scantily clad girl with her arms entwined around the neck of a half-naked man lay on a leopard skin bedspread. She gave a groan of disappointment. She had read it before.

The Naked Image had sold millions after it was nominated by the Book of the Month Club in America, and had been on the best-seller list all over the world. It had recently been turned into a multi-million dollar film in Hollywood, and its author, Drake Janess, was supposed to be having an affair with Celia Manners, the film's leading lady. What a combination! She the latest sex-goddess, and he the perfect disciple!

Out of boredom, Emma browsed through it again. The plot was excellent and the torrid love scenes were vividly described. Yet there was a cynicism and worldliness about the book that she disliked, and she soon let it lie on the coverlet and allowed her thoughts to drift to her employer.

His parents were obviously wealthy, but from what he had said, he did not derive his income from their business. What did he do that they found so distasteful? He spent a considerable time in his small study, and she assumed he was dictating letters, because when the door was ajar she had noticed a tape recorder perched on the desk.

Everything about him interested her, in a way that Peter never had. His very presence in the room was exciting, and even in her weakened state a shiver of pleasure had run through her body as she had seen him standing by her bed. A golden Viking. Her first impression of him had not changed, and she was ruefully aware that neither had his!

Yet why should he see her as anything other than his temporary cook? From what he had said, he enjoyed women when it suited him, and never let himself become seriously involved. Bearing this in mind, it would be foolish and dangerous to read anything into his friendly camaraderie.

Her eyes began to close, and although she jerked herself up a couple of times in the hope that she would be awake if Jake Sanders came in to say goodnight, she did not manage to do so, and within a short time was sound asleep.

Emma did not see her employer on Friday, although Carmen assured her that he had enquired after her. She felt much better, even though she still looked a sight. Her whole body was peeling in huge ugly flakes; even her lips, which had dried and cracked, were in the same unhappy state, and her hair looked dank and lifeless.

At least she could do something about that. She ran a very cool bath and gratefully sank into it, washing her hair at the same time and then towelling it dry before she pinned it back into the severe style she had adopted since coming here.

The day passed swiftly. Carmen cooked her a large omelette for lunch and then she slept for most of the afternoon, and after an early supper she found some cards in her case and played Patience until she could no longer keep her eyes open.

For the next three days Emma only saw Carmen. Jake Sanders was out most of the time, only popping his head round the door of her room to enquire if she was all right. She supposed he had many friends on the island, and imagined him surrounded by a bevy of beautiful women, all of them tall and blonde.

It was a relief for her to start work again on Monday morning, especially when Jake came in after breakfast to pay her first week's salary.

'I'd prefer not to accept it,' she said, turning from the sink to look at him. 'I've done very little to earn it this week.'

'Nonsense! You didn't burn yourself on purpose. And you'll be kept damned busy once my guests arrive.'

She could see from his set expression that he did not wish to argue the matter, and she guiltily put the money in her apron pocket.

'May I use the car tomorrow morning?' she asked, as he turned to leave. 'Carmen has agreed to get here early and take me to the shops.'

'Yes, but don't take the Mercedes. I keep a small Datsun here as well, and you can use it any time you like.'

'Don't you trust me with the Mercedes?' she couldn't resist asking.

'I'm not even sure I trust you with the Datsun!'

She sniffed. He was making no attempt to be polite.

'I happen to be an excellent driver,' she informed him.

'Better than you are a cook?'

Emma bit hard on her lip.

'Remember to keep to the right,' he went on.

'I'll switch on the engine too. I'm not stupid, Mr Sanders.'

Suddenly he smiled, and her heart turned over. Quickly she faced the sink again, alarmed by her reaction to him. Misinterpreting her gesture for one of anger, he said contritely:

'I'm sorry, Emma. It's mean of me to tease you. We'll forget your sunburn and the ruined dinner, *and* my ruined slacks, and begin again. After all, things can only get better—I hope!'

He sauntered out and Emma busied herself preparing lunch and dinner, taking great pains to ensure that both meals were well balanced as to taste, and appealing to the eye.

After her employer had finished his cheese and onion quiche at lunch, he wandered down to the pool, and Emma, observing him through the kitchen window, decided this might be an opportune moment to return the book Carmen had borrowed for her.

His library-cum-study was an appealing room with

deep easy chairs, masses of records and tapes and shelf upon shelf of books. There were several by Drake Janess and a new novel of his which she had not even heard of. Curiously she picked it up and browsed through the synopsis on the flyleaf.

'Enjoying it?' a voice asked behind her.

Startled, she spun round and saw her employer pad into the room.

'It looks as trashy as his others,' she replied.

'I thought *The Naked Image* was rather good,' he said. 'It had excellent reviews.'

'I found it too cynical,' she replied. 'And also too—er—too lurid.'

'You mean too sexy?'

'Yes.'

'That figures.'

She ignored the comment. 'I've not seen a review of this new one.'

'It's not out in England yet. I got this in New York a couple of months ago.'

'I'm surprised you've read it.'

'Why? I happen to think Drake Janess has a great deal of talent.'

'You don't have to be talented to write about sex,' she expostulated scornfully.

'He has first class plots too.'

Although Emma agreed, she was determined not to admit it. 'They're very predictable.'

'Several million people disagree with you! *The Naked Image* has been a runaway best seller.'

'It can't run away far enough, if you ask me!'

'I hope for the author's sake that no one ever does.'

Puzzled by his defence of the man, Emma softened her tone. 'I know I sound a bit high-handed, but it makes me furious when I see this sort of book getting the breaks, while wonderful writers sometimes have to struggle for years.'

'How do you know *he* didn't struggle for years?'

'Because I've read his publicity. He more or less admitted he deliberately set out to write a best-seller—and he knew the right ingredients.'

'They're the same ingredients that went into books like *Wuthering Heights*, *Jane Eyre*, *Anna Karenina*, and many other classics. The only difference is that Janess brings it up to date with modern plots.'

'You're not comparing him with the Brontës or Tolstoy, I hope?'

He gave a wry grin. 'Even *I* wouldn't be that sacrilegious! No, I was merely trying to make my point.'

'I'm sure he'd be overwhelmed just to hear his name *mentioned* in such illustrious company. *He's* nothing more than a sexploiting hack. Writers like the Brontës or Jane Austen or Tolstoy speak of love—but Janess only writes about lust.'

'An emotion you've never felt, I assume?'

'That's beside the point. We're not discussing *my* love-life.'

'Have you got one?' His tone ridiculed her. 'I'd be surprised if you had.'

'How dare you say that? You know nothing about me.'

'I know enough to realise how narrow-minded you are.'

'I don't think it's narrow to despise Drake Janess's exaggerations and lies.'

'What lies?'

'His love scenes,' she stated. 'No ordinary woman achieves the ecstasy of his heroines.'

'How do *you* know? On your own admission you're a virgin!'

There was no answer to this, and she reddened. But she

was still not ready to give in. 'How do *you* know what women feel?'

'They tell me—and I can see for myself. Like this,' he added, pulling her swiftly into his arms and pressing his mouth to hers.

Instantly she was conscious of his near-naked body, clad only in the briefest of swimming trunks. The firm muscles of his thighs pressed against her own and his mouth was warm and demanding as he forced her lips apart. She tried to resist, but in spite of her anger, she responded and, as he became aware of it, his kiss deepened and became more intimate. Never had she been kissed with such intensity or expertise. His hands moved over her breasts, lightly caressing them until they hardened at his touch, the nipples rising and tingling with a sensation she had never before experienced. Desire flooded through her and her legs felt weak. She wanted him to go on kissing her, and was deeply mortified when he abruptly released her and stepped back.

'I think I've made my point,' he said triumphantly.

She glared at him. 'In a very despicable way, Mr Sanders. You had no right to touch me! I'm here as your cook—nothing more.'

'Don't worry, I've no intention of trying to change your status. If you're as clumsy in bed as you are in the kitchen——'

'How dare you! I may be inexperienced, but I——'

'*So* inexperienced that it might be better if you confined your reading to Mickey Mouse!'

Emma glared at him even more angrily. If he had not been her employer she would have slapped his face. That would wipe the smirk from it! Before she could think of a suitable retort, he walked on to the patio and disappeared from view.

But the hurt of his remark remained with her. She knew

he had only kissed her to prove his point, but her passionate response had warned her of the danger inherent in the situation. She dared not let it happen again. Not because she didn't want it to, but because she wanted it too much.

Drat that idiot Drake Janess! If it had not been for him, none of this would have happened.

Perhaps she *had* sounded narrow and prissy—but that had not been her intention. Jake Sanders brought out the worst in her, and they were on a constant collision course—although she had to admit that this was one collision she had enjoyed!

She put her hands to her lips. Peter had never aroused her in this way. Nor had he ever kissed her so intimately. But at least his kisses meant something, which was not the case where her employer was concerned.

Carmen looked up from polishing the cupboards as Emma came into the kitchen. 'I forgot ask. You enjoy book?'

'I'd read it before.'

'You like?'

'Not much.'

'Please, you no tell Mr Sanders.'

'I already have.'

For an instant Carmen was motionless, then she burst into laughter, her plump body shaking with it.

Emma was puzzled. 'What have I said that's so funny?'

Carmen's face sobered, though her eyes still danced with amusement. 'Mr Sanders—he write.'

'*What?* You don't . . . *oh no*! Mr Sanders can't be Drake Janess?'

'He are. I no tell before because I want give you surprise after you read.'

Emma's heart sank. Carmen had certainly given her a surprise, but one she could have well done without! Life here was one disaster after another, and this time she had put both feet in it. No wonder his reaction to her criticisms had been so hostile! She went through each word but, try as she would, could not find one redeeming remark. She must go out and apologise at once.

Taking her courage in both hands, she walked down to the pool, where he was seated under an umbrella correcting a manuscript.

'Yes?' he asked coldly.

'I owe you an apology Mr Sanders. If I'd known you were Drake Janess, I would never have spoken as I did.'

'Naturally,' he answered. 'I suppose Carmen told you?'

She nodded. 'But why didn't *you* tell me, instead of letting me make a fool of myself?'

'You needed no help from me on that score,' he replied curtly. 'You've managed to do that with alarming regularity since you arrived here.'

'Thanks for being so understanding!'

'It's fortunate that I am,' he replied. 'Otherwise you might be packing your bags at this moment.' He glanced down at the papers on his lap. 'I'm working on the screenplay of my new piece of rubbish, and I'm already behind schedule, so if you don't mind. . . .'

Emma stalked off, furious at his curt treatment. He could at least have accepted her apology with better grace.

Carmen took one look at her crestfallen face and realised what had happened. 'He very angry, no?'

'He very angry, yes!'

'I sorry, Emma. Is my fault.'

Emma shrugged. 'I should have sensed something was wrong when he got so annoyed. But I just carried on making things worse. I wouldn't mind betting I've seen his photograph dozens of times in the papers, but because of his beard I didn't recognise him.'

'He grow this year. He very handsome with it.'

'And very handsome without it,' Emma replied. 'Isn't he engaged to the girl who starred in his film?'

'He tell me no, and she tell me yes.'

'What's she like?'

Carmen shrugged. 'I no like, my daughters no like, but all mens like. She come here soon, and you have plenty work. Miss Manners very fussy lady.'

Emma pondered on this bit of information for the rest of the afternoon. What a devastatingly handsome couple her employer and Miss Manners must make! Well, that settled her own hash. Any ideas she had entertained of attracting him could be kissed goodbye with that kind of competition!

But at least dinner turned out to be a great success, and Jake grudgingly came into the kitchen to tell her so.

'You really can cook!' His voice held a strong element of surprise. 'The cream sauce on the veal was delicious. What flavouring did you use?'

'Nutmeg,' she replied. 'I even put a pinch of it in the prawn soufflé.'

'That was like a feather.' He eyed her. 'Now, how about joining me for coffee?'

'No, thanks.'

'Are you still annoyed with me for kissing you? It didn't mean a thing, you know, and it won't happen again.'

How well she understood *that*. Wasn't that the main reason for her anger? 'I haven't given it another thought,' she lied. 'But I've a headache, and as I have to be up early in the morning. . . .'

'Ah, a headache,' he said understandingly. 'Commonly referred to as "woman's salvation"!'

He strolled back to the lounge, where she heard him pick up the telephone, and shortly afterwards he drove away.

Moodily Emma retired to her room. It had been childish not to have accepted his olive branch. If she were to stay here for the next few months there was no point in bearing any animosity.

What had she really been afraid of? Her own feelings when she was close to him? Yes, she had to admit that she found him too attractive. And it hurt unbearably to know that he did not find her equally so. Yet how could he, when she had done her best to make herself look unattractive?

Damn! Why couldn't she have found a job with a family? Before she arrived in Majorca her life had been uncomplicated. Now her feelings were troubled and impossible to sort out clearly.

CHAPTER FOUR

After a restless night, Emma was relieved to see dawn breaking, and she was down long before Carmen arrived.

She browsed through the storage cupboards and made a list of everything she needed, and soon after breakfast they set off in the bright red Datsun for Paguera.

The bustling village surprised her. It was lively without being too noisy, and as they drove along the front she glimpsed the sandy, sheltered cove of Paguera's beach. Along the main road which faced the sea, there were many souvenir shops and boutiques, as well as several supermarkets, and they made their way to the largest. Most of the branded goods were the same as in England, and prices were not dissimilar, apart from butter and coffee which were considerably dearer. Fortunately money was not a problem for her, and soon her wire trolley was full. A young man carried out the boxes and they next made their way to the small market for fresh fruit and vegetables.

The assortment was as excellent as the quality, and Emma enjoyed being able to pick out the large firm tomatoes and ripe golden peaches before the assistant placed them in a bag for weighing.

'For big shopping Mr Sanders like you go Palma. Meat better there. Big market, big choice,' Carmen told her as they made their way back home again.

'How do I get there?' Emma asked. 'And will it be easy to find the market? I believe Palma's quite large.'

The older woman patted her hand reassuringly. 'I go with you first time. You no worry.'

Driving slowly along, Emma admired the pine trees and cliffs that lined the shore, while Carmen told her that Paguera had originally been a fishing village. Now it was a prosperous town and the main hotel, the Villamil, was British owned, though built in the style of a Spanish castle.

Emma stopped the Datsun outside the front entrance and told Carmen they would have a coffee here.

The woman looked horrified. 'I never been. I no dressed.'

'Neither am I, but I'm sure it won't matter.' Before the reluctant woman could protest again, Emma urged her out of the car.

The hotel was comfortably furnished and directly overlooked the beach. The shaded gardens had a small swimming pool, and already there were several children playing in it.

They seated themselves at a small table under an umbrella, and within moments a waiter appeared to take their order.

They sipped their coffee in silence. Carmen was obviously overawed by her surroundings, and Emma gladly listened to the chatter of other people. It made her realise how lonely it was at the villa. Her conversations with Carmen were limited, as they had been with her employer, and unless she made an effort to go out when she could, the long periods of silence might get her down.

On her way back to the car, she stopped to buy some postcards and stamps at the hall desk. She had telephoned her grandparents the day after her arrival, but she knew they were waiting to receive a letter, as was Peter. She dreaded their reaction when they learned she was sharing a villa with a single man, and wondered how best to gloss over it without actually lying.

'We late,' Carmen announced as they drove along the stony unmade road towards the villa. 'Mr Sanders no have breakfast.'

'I know. But I had to stop for coffee. My head was splitting.'

Entering the kitchen a few moments later, arms full of parcels, Emma saw Jake Sanders leaning against the fridge, sipping a glass of orange juice.

'I'm sorry to be late,' she apologised. 'I'll get your breakfast right away.'

'I don't want anything more than juice,' he replied irritably. 'I had a late night and too much to drink.' He moved towards the patio. 'Come outside, will you, please. It's too hot to talk in here.'

She followed him, leaving Carmen to put the food away, and he motioned her to sit down.

'I'm giving a dinner party on Friday,' he went on, 'and I'd like you to draw up a menu and let me see it.'

'How many guests are you expecting?'

'Eight.'

'Is it a formal dinner?'

'Well, I don't want a sandwich and Coke evening!'

She did not smile. 'I meant are the people close friends

of yours or do you want to *impress* them?'

'I like to impress my *friends* too,' he said, deliberately misunderstanding her. 'So come up with something unusual and elaborate, but not too rich. The ladies are dieting.' He half turned away from her. 'I don't want any lunch. Just leave me to work undisturbed. I must get on with this script.'

The first thing Emma did after clearing away the breakfast things was to consult her cookery books and plan the menu. Pensively she rummaged among the pages. After several false starts she wrote out her choice on a sheet of paper. She would wait until this evening to show it to her employer; as he had seemed adamant about being left alone during the day.

Because he was seated by the pool, she skirted it and made her way down to the beach for a swim. Her sunburn had completely cleared and her skin was back to normal, but she heeded the doctor's advice and only sat out for half an hour, and then lay underneath the shade of a tree, drowsing in the heat of the sun.

When she returned, Jake Sanders was still working at the poolside, and did not even look up as she approached.

Emma cleared her throat to attract his attention and he looked up.

'May I take the car after dinner and go to Paguera?' she asked hesitantly.

'I told you that you can have the car whenever you want.'

'I didn't realise you meant it was for my personal use as well, Mr Sanders,' she answered stiffly.

'I wish you'd stop acting like the servant of a wicked master,' he said impatiently.

Her silence spoke volumes and he sighed gustily.

'This is the twentieth century, Emma. We're equals, and my name is Jake.'

She remained silent and he frowned at her.

'Calling me by my first name won't alter our relationship. You'll still be quite safe with me.'

'I'm not frightened.'

'Aren't you? Then why do you slink past me like a petrified cat, and why do you look at me as if I'm going to bite you any minute?'

'Because you're often bad-tempered and in a biting mood,' she retorted. 'The way you are now.'

There was a short silence, broken at last by a soft chuckle.

'You're quite right, Emma, I *am* a bad-tempered devil. But only because I'm working flat out. Maybe a rest will do me good, and by way of apologising to you, how about letting *me* feed *you* tomorrow evening? We'll go out somewhere.'

She was astounded. 'You're asking me to have dinner with you?'

'Why not? Regard it as the pipe of peace. Well?'

'I'd love to,' she answered.

'That's settled, then.'

He turned back to his script and Emma went up to her room with a spring in her step.

Why had Jake suddenly changed from a bear to a lamb? After all, he had engaged her as a cook, and had no reason to treat her other than as a member of his staff. Asking her out was more than she could possibly have hoped for.

As soon as dinner was over, Emma made her way to Paguera. Driving on the right-hand side of the road presented no problems, even in the dark, and she parked along the front and sauntered with the throngs of tanned holidaymakers, enjoying the balmy night air. The cafés were packed, but she managed to find an empty seat in the corner of a seedy-looking bar, where she sat nervously sipping a lemonade, until she was forced to leave by the unwanted attentions of two middle-aged Romeos.

It was not much fun being on your own, she thought enviously, as she watched laughing couples walk by. With no one to talk to, she soon tired of her own company, and she gladly turned the car around for the homeward journey.

Jake was in the kitchen making himself some coffee when she came in.

'You're back early,' he remarked.

'I thought I'd write some letters home.' Emma took the percolator from him and set out the cups. Jake perched on a chair and watched her.

'Missing your boy-friend?' he asked.

'One of the reasons I took this job was to get away from him, so that I could make up my mind whether to marry him.'

'Ah yes. I remember you telling me you weren't sure whether you loved him. What's the problem? Waiting to be swept off your feet by a knight in shining armour?'

She glimpsed her face in the little mosaic-edged mirror that Carmen had put beside the freezer, and bit back a smile at the sight of her ludicrously pencilled eyebrows. 'With my looks, that's hardly likely to happen.'

'Don't belittle yourself, Emma. You would be quite attractive if you did something with yourself. You've got a beautiful body, although you hide it with those awful smocks you seem to favour, and you put on your make-up so badly that I'm beginning to suspect you do it on purpose.'

Colour stained her cheeks. 'Why should I do that?'

'Beats me. Unless. . . .' He suddenly grinned. 'Of course! You were scared witless when you found out we were going to be alone in the villa. So you figured if you looked a mess, you'd be safe from my male lust.'

'You're talking nonsense,' she declared. 'I'm not at all

scared of being alone with you.'

'Not now you know me,' he said. 'But you were in the beginning. Own up, Emma.'

'Well . . . perhaps I was. But definitely not now.'

'Thank God for that! So no more funny eyebrows and scrimped-back hair, eh?'

She nodded, unexpectedly shy as she poured the coffee and passed him a cup.

'And no spectacles, either,' he added. 'You've got lovely eyes. I noticed them the night you were ill.'

'I can't see without glasses,' she said quickly, afraid to ponder on what else he had seen.

'Try contact lenses. They're fantastic.'

'I've got some,' she admitted, 'but I'm too lazy to persevere with them.'

'You *must*,' he ordered. 'I wear them all the time.'

She looked at him with astonishment. 'You're short-sighted as well?'

'If I took them out and Bo Derek walked naked in front of me, I wouldn't even blush!'

She took off her glasses and looked straight at him. 'If that's the case, there's only one way to make sure I do persevere.' Swiftly she flung her spectacles on to the tiled floor. They immediately shattered, and Jake gave such a roar of appreciation that she dared not tell him she had another pair safely tucked away in a drawer upstairs!

'Good for you!' he said admiringly, and came to stand beside her. He was so tall that she felt like a midget beside him. 'That was a spunky thing to do, Emma. But will you be able to find your way to your room now, or do you need a guide-dog?'

She backed away from him. 'I may be half-sighted Jake, but I'm not half-witted!'

He chuckled. 'You're never lost for an answer, are you?'

Emma accepted the compliment with a smile. 'Will you excuse me now? I'd like to get my letters written. It's a chore I hate, and the sooner I do it the better.'

'My sentiments entirely. If I'd been bothered to write a longer reply to you, you'd still be in Oakton, happy with your lot.'

'I'd made up my mind to leave the village regardless of whether I got this job.'

'Instead of which you flew out to cook for Jane Sanders and found she was the playboy author of a sexy best-seller!'

'If my grandparents had known who you were, they'd never have let me come,' she confessed.

'Aren't you old enough to do as you please?'

'Old enough, but not selfish enough. I wouldn't want to upset them.'

'What will you do if they ask you to come back?'

She decided to be honest. 'I don't intend telling them the whole truth. I'll say your brother and his family are down here already. By the time they reply that will be true.'

Jake did not hide his amusement. 'Haven't you even lived away from home before?'

'Only when I was training in London. And then I stayed with some elderly relations.'

'You're really something else!' he said in wonderment. 'Haven't you heard of Women's Lib in your neck of the woods? You talk as if you're still living between the pages of Jane Austen!'

'Unfortunately my grandparents still are.'

'Do you always do everything to please them? Supposing you wanted to marry a man they didn't approve of?'

'That's extremely unlikely.'

'How do you know?' His eyes twinkled. 'Take me, for

instance. Would they approve of me as a husband?'

Emma felt herself blushing. 'They'd approve of your family.'

'That's a coward's answer!'

'It's a diplomat's one!' she smiled.

'Clever little girl.'

His tone was paternalistic, and she was depressingly aware that he still saw her as a child.

'How about a swim before you write your letters?' he suggested unexpectedly.

'Are you serious?'

'Why not? It's almost as warm now as it is in the shade during the day.'

She hesitated, shy of swimming alone with him in the dark, even though the pool was floodlit.

'Come on,' he urged. 'It will all be perfectly respectable. No skinny-dipping, and any time I get a lewd thought, I'll close my eyes and think of your grandma!'

Provoked by his teasing, Emma went to her room to change. After putting in her contact lenses, having twice tripped on the stairs—she slipped on her black school costume. Unfortunately she had still not bought another one, and it was extremely unflattering. But it would have to do. In fact it was a darn sight safer than a bikini.

Jake was waiting by the pool for her, and roared with laughter as she approached.

'I've never seen anyone swim in a shroud before! That costume of yours is better than an ice-cold shower for turning a man off!'

'It's my school costume.' For two pins she would have gone back to her room and let him swim alone.

'Is that so? I thought you'd found it in a coffin!'

It was impossible not to laugh. 'Actually I've been meaning to buy a new one since I arrived,' she explained, 'but I keep forgetting.'

'Don't bother on my account. I know all about your hidden virtues!'

She went scarlet. 'That's hitting below the belt. I thought you'd be gentlemanly enough not to refer to it.'

'I can assure you it was not below the belt I was thinking of! Is that gentlemanly enough for you?'

Awarding him the best of the exchange, Emma responded by giving him a hefty shove into the water. As he fell, he caught hold of her wrist, and dragged her in with him, and laughingly ducked her under as she came to the surface.

She swam the length of the pool underwater, and then crawled leisurely to the far end, while Jake churned up several lengths at breakneck speed.

Holding on to the tiled surround, Emma paused to catch her breath, and allowed her feet to float upwards to the surface, her hair splayed out behind her in strands of shiny brown silk. Then she closed her eyes and let go, floating gently along, carried by Jake's wake as he completed his umpteenth length.

With a sudden lithe movement he heaved himself from the water and stood on the edge, skin glistening like polished mahogany in the floodlighting, his hair darker now that it was wet. He was better looking than any film star, she thought with a pang, and wished she could hold his interest. But she had no chance. With his looks and success, he was the target for some of the loveliest looking girls in the world.

'What are you thinking?'

Taken by surprise at his question, she nearly blurted out the truth, but stopped herself in time. 'I feel as if I'm playing truant from school,' she lied. 'I should be writing letters, but instead I'm enjoying myself.'

'I'm sure you were far too obedient to have ever played truant, Emma. Unlike me, that is. I even ran away from boarding school twice.'

'A rebel without a cause,' she murmured.

'But I did have a cause,' he contradicted, and sat down on the edge next to her. 'I loathed boarding school. Some children do, you know, but the British system doesn't make allowances for them. My father went to my old school and his father before him. His attitude was, if they liked it, why the hell shouldn't I? My parents didn't understand me from a very early age.'

'At least it makes a change from the old chestnut about the wife!'

He looked at her blankly for a moment, then laughed. 'I'll never offer *that* as an excuse. A wife is one appendage I won't have.'

'How can you be so sure?'

'I'm thirty-three, Emma. Old enough to know my own mind. I love women—too much to tie myself to one.'

'Did you eventually stay in boarding school?'

Her change of conversation took him by surprise, but he saw she had done it deliberately, and was amused. 'Yes,' he said, 'and I surprised everyone by winning a scholarship to Oxford.'

'What did you read?'

'Need you ask, having read my book! English, of course! That's why I have such a mastery of the language!'

She laughed. 'I really did put my foot in it, didn't I? I was awfully upset when Carmen told me your identity.'

'Forget it, child. Your honesty is one of your main attractions.'

Emma appreciated his comment, though not his calling her a child. 'It's only because I'm five feet one,' she stated.

'I beg your pardon?'

'Why you called me child,' she explained. 'You wouldn't if I were taller.'

He eyed her, moving slowly over her body. 'A beautiful child,' he murmured. 'Tiny, but perfect in every detail.'

Hurriedly Emma stood up and wrapped herself in the large towel she had brought down with her.

'I think I'll go up now. I really must get my letters done.'

This time he made no effort to stop her, and she padded away, keeping her steps slow and resisting the urge to run.

Her letters were easier to compose than she had expected. She managed several pages to her grandparents, and a short note to Peter, telling them of Jake's true identity, and also explaining about the mix-up at the airport. She made this passage as long and amusing as she could, and glossed over the details about his family staying at the villa. She hated lying, but in the circumstances it was preferable to the truth. She sealed the envelopes with relief, and then hastily scrawled a few postcards to various friends.

Her room seemed particularly hot and stuffy this evening, and she walked out on the balcony and leaned, chin in hand, on the railings to stare into the night.

The full moon beamed down, reflecting its silver light on the distant sea, wine dark now, while a faint breeze stirred the trees. The silence was total: even the cicadas had stopped their incessant cheeping.

How happy she felt at this moment. Jake had behaved quite differently towards her this evening, and although she wondered at it, she could not think of any ulterior motive that he could have for being so nice to her. There was no doubt she was flattered by his attentions—what girl wouldn't be? But was it foolish to read too much into it? By tomorrow he might regret his familiarity and return to their more formal relationship.

Yet tomorrow they were going out for dinner together. It was unbelievable. The thought of spending an entire evening alone with him made her heart race wildly. Would he try to kiss her when they were alone in the car, and would she resist him if he did? Emma already knew the answer to that question, and she turned and went back into her room.

In a few minute she was asleep.

It was while she was making the mayonnaise for the crab salad she was serving for lunch that Jake came into the kitchen.

'I thought we'd go into Palma fairly early this afternoon,' he said. 'I have to go to the bank and I'll be there about an hour, so if you want to look around the shops, it will give you the opportunity.'

'That would be lovely.'

'Jake.'

'What?'

'That would be lovely, Jake,' he said. 'That's my name. I thought you'd agreed to use it.'

She blushed. 'Of course—Jake.'

'That's better. Be ready by three, Emma.'

Emma was ready promptly to time. Although she still wore her hair scraped back from her face, she no longer applied her make-up badly, knowing Jake would see it as fear if she did. But neither did she do anything to enhance her looks, not wishing him to think she was trying to entice him. She did take some care over her choice of clothes, however, discarding her old ones in favour of a new outfit—navy French jeans with a white cotton shirt.

'Well, well,' Jake commented, as he helped her into the Mercedes. 'So the maternity smocks have finally gone! You should wear trousers more often—you have the figure for them.'

They drove along the coast road at breakneck speed for the first half of the journey, but then Jake slowed down to give her the opportunity of appreciating the scenery, which in parts was extremely pretty.

'The other side of the island is much more spectacular,' he explained as they glimpsed an empty cove set among pines and shrub-covered rocks. 'I'll take you there one day next week, and we'll have lunch at Formentor.'

Soon they had passed the promenade of Palma Nova with its tree-lined gardens, and entered Magaluf with its long curving beach. It was a bustling resort, and the wooded hills behind added a splash of green to the bright sunny landscape.

'You should have seen this place fifteen years ago,' Jake remarked as they were held up by a traffic jam in the town's narrow main road. 'I first came down here when I was eighteen, and I was doing Europe for six months before going up to Oxford. There were only two hotels here and the beach was almost deserted. Now look at it!' He could not keep the disgust out of his voice, and indeed it was difficult to envisage the resort in its unspoiled state. The magnificent beach was thronged with holidaymakers as far as the eye could see, and the pavements outside the shops were packed with tanned bodies fighting for space.

The sun beat down on their heads as they sat in the open air, and as Emma wiped some beads of perspiration from her forehead, Jake noticed. He pressed a button on the dashboard, and slowly the hood of the Mercedes rose and covered the car, and then a moment later he flicked another switch and the air-conditioning came on.

'I think I'll leave the hood up for the time being. We're liable to hit a lot of traffic all the way in now. This is the time that most people go shopping.'

Palma was dominated by its ancient Gothic cathedral, which was perched high above on a hill, and could be seen from almost any part of the town. As they drove along the wide, tree-lined promenade that led to the main boulevards, they stopped for a moment to admire the magnificent array of yachts moored in the large harbour. Nearby in the docks stood an enormous cruise ship, its hull gleaming white, with bunting flying in the slight breeze, while American battleships of the Sixth Fleet flanked it on either side.

Jake pointed out the church of San Francisco that stood beside the cathedral and told her the history of the nearby gold and white castle of Bellvar as he manoeuvred his car into a space on the pavement outside a large bank in the town centre.

'Won't you get fined for leaving it here?' Emma asked, noticing the No Parking signs written in several languages.

'The local bobby on this beat knows me, and he's a very understanding man.'

He came round to help her out, and they stood among the milling throng as he pointed out directions.

'I'll meet you back here in an hour, and then we'll go into one of the hotels for a drink before we eat.'

She was about to turn away, when he stopped her. 'Have you enough money? I can always give you an advance if you're short.'

She shook her head. 'Thanks, but I've plenty in pesetas as well as travellers' cheques.'

'Make sure you're not diddled on the exchange rate, and if you're in any doubt, wait for me and I'll go back with you. Sometimes they pretend not to understand the language when it suits them, and it always comes as a bit of a shock to find an Englishman who speaks Spanish fluently.'

With a wave he disappeared into the marble portals of the bank, and Emma stood on the pavement at a loss, undecided whether to turn to the right or the left.

CHAPTER FIVE

An hour was not very long to see the town, so she stuck to the turnings nearest the square. The shops were well stocked with fashionable goods, particularly suede and leather, and much cheaper than at home. She had over a hundred pounds on her, and she had no compunctions about spending it all. She sorely needed beachwear, and entered the first boutique that stocked it. Within ten minutes she had purchased two bikinis with matching skirts, and with a shock she realised they had taken up almost all of her money.

As she emerged with her packages into the bright sunlight her eyes were immediately caught by a hairdressers. If only she had time to have her hair done as well, but it was impossible in the half hour she had left to her. Instead, she stepped into a hotel and made for the cloakroom, where she pulled her hair free of its pins and ran a comb through the silky tresses.

Pleased with herself, she retraced her steps to the car, and found Jake leaning nonchalantly against the bonnet, just as he was the first night he had met her. He did not see her, and she had a good opportunity to study him. She noticed that the heads of nearly every woman—young and old—turned to look at him as they passed by, and she was in no way surprised. Clad in a dazzling white silk shirt, open at the neck, and tight-fitting black slacks, he cut a handsome and dashing figure.

As she drew nearer, he turned and saw her. For a long moment he surveyed her, his face devoid of expression, then he sauntered over to relieve her of some of her packages.

'You certainly took advantage of that hour, by the looks of it,' he commented, his eyes on the parcels as he opened the boot. His hand brushed hers and the touch of long, tapering fingers sent a sharp thrill through her body.

He straightened, and his eyebrows lifted quizzically. 'I'm glad you took notice of what I said to you last night. You look a different person today.'

'Clothes maketh woman,' she answered.

'So does normal make-up.' His eyes gleamed. 'Apart from the fact that you felt safer being one of the Ugly Sisters, were you paying me back for eyeing all the lovelies at the airport the night I was waiting for you?'

'Certainly not!' she said indignantly. 'How you live your life is your affair—and so are your affairs! Though now I think of it, you did say you didn't want a cook who was in any way presentable. So all I did was comply!'

He laughed and helped her into the car, then set it in motion. 'I didn't mean you to take me so literally,' he said finally.

'I don't any more.'

'Except for last night,' he teased.

'Only because I was getting fed up with my own image each time I looked at myself!'

'So was I. So don't change back into a frog, will you?'

She giggled. 'That was Prince Charming's disguise.'

'There's no sex discrimination allowed now—so it could be Princess Charming's too.'

She giggled again. 'How charming *you* are, Jake. I'm not used to it. When do you start being your old frank and rude self again?'

'Never rude,' he countered. 'At least only rarely. But often too damn frank. It's made me a lot of enemies. People prefer sycophants.'

'I don't agree,' she protested. 'I don't approve of frankness that's cruel; but when it means honesty and no prevarication, then I'm all for it. The only trouble is that most outspoken people aren't too keen on receiving the same treatment. They usually take offence!'

'Is that a warning for me?'

'Perhaps.'

'Exercising some of that tact, are you?'

'Only until I get to know you better.' She flashed him a look from beneath her lashes. 'I never like to judge a book by its cover.'

'Unless it's one of mine, that is!'

She laughed, and they drove along in silence until they started to climb above the town into the countryside. Soon they came to the Son Vida estate, with its luxurious villas built in the extensive grounds of the hotel, and the eighteen-hole golf course, kept verdant green by the constant spray of hundreds of tiny jets of water. As they drew up at the entrance of the hotel, a porter immediately opened the car door for them, and taking the keys from Jake, whom he knew, parked the car.

They walked through the marble-floored hall out to the magnificent gardens, and strolled around admiringly, ending up at the huge swimming pool, where they sat on wrought iron chairs and ordered drinks.

'What a peaceful place,' Emma remarked contentedly as she sipped a San Francisco, a concoction of fruit juices flavoured with grenadine.

'I'm glad you like it,' Jake replied. 'I have friends with homes in the grounds and I often come here, but it's always nice to see it through the eyes of a stranger.'

'I'm still surprised you enjoy living in Majorca. Sun and sea are fine for a few months, but I'd have thought it would be dull on a year-round basis.'

'I don't stay here all year,' he explained. 'As soon as I get restless I take off for Los Angeles or New York, or wherever my fancy takes me. I only use the villa as a base.'

'Don't you ever come to England to see your parents?'

'Twice a year, but I rarely stay more than a few days. After that we usually end up arguing.'

Emma longed to know what about, but lacked the nerve to ask him. However, her curiosity was satisfied, when he continued to speak, his tone musing, almost as if he were talking to himself.

'They dislike my life-style mainly. They'd like me to get married, give up my writing and go into the family business. The fact that I've already made more money than my father or grandfather put together fails to move them—although money is the thing that impresses them most in others.'

'Why are they so against your writing?' It was a question Emma felt she could ask without it looking as if she were prying.

'It's not writing in general,' he said, 'so much as what I write. They'd prefer it if I sold three thousand copies of an esoteric book that no one except a handful of intellectual snobs could understand—rather than three million copies that the general public can love. You're the same.'

'I'm not,' Emma protested. 'I enjoy popular novels. It's just that yours . . . yours worry me. There's a bluntness and harshness about them that I find disturbing.'

'Because you live in a dream world where good always conquers bad, and evil people always get their come-uppance.' There was a pause. 'To be honest,' he suddenly admitted, 'I only wrote *The Naked Image* as a joke, because I was tired of trying to flog my other books. I'd written three before that one—all serious and soul-searching—and had them all rejected.'

'Truly?' She was amazed.

'Truly,' he smiled. 'I realised there was money to be

made writing big, sexy novels, so I've exploited it to the full. Now I refuse to knock it. If it's what people want, who am I to disagree?'

So that was the real reason he had been so offended by her remarks. They echoed his own guilty thoughts which he preferred to keep buried.

'Are you still keen to write a different kind of book?' she asked carefully.

'Not for the moment. I prefer to enjoy my ill-gotten gains, and churn out more along the same line. Besides, my public expect me to keep to the same formula, and I wouldn't like to disappoint them!'

She stared into his blue eyes. They were unwavering as they gazed into her own.

'Disappointed that I don't have ambitions for immortality?' he asked.

'Your life isn't over yet, Jake. One day I'm sure you'll astonish your public with a book that's totally different—and they'll go overboard for it.'

'Funny little thing, aren't you?' he drawled. 'You'd really be happy if I'd said I wanted to become an intellectual writer.'

'It has nothing to do with that. But you have a sharp, good mind, and you could make the world sit up and take notice. You know the old adage,' she went on lightly. 'The pen is mightier than the sword.'

'I prefer *my* adage,' he countered. 'A little money is better than a lot of reputation!'

She made a protesting face. 'Aren't you ever serious?'

'Not when I'm with a pretty girl.' He nodded to her drink. 'How about a refill?'

'I'd love one.'

They sat in silence while the waiter mixed them, and Emma gave thought to their discussion. Despite what he said about his parents, she was convinced that their disapproval of him hurt him. Perhaps if he married a girl whom they liked, it would make them less critical of his books? Thank heavens her own grandparents didn't confuse loving her with approving of everything she did!

'Come back to me, Emma,' Jake drawled as the waiter set down the fresh glasses. 'You seem miles away.'

'I was thinking of our first meeting,' she lied. 'It's funny that I didn't recognise you. You've had so much publicity—especially when it was rumoured that you might be marrying Celia Manners.'

'That was only a ruse to promote the film,' he shrugged. 'She's the hottest box-office property at the moment, and the studio dreamed up the whole idea.'

Emma's spirits lifted. 'You mean it isn't true?'

'I won't marry *anyone*,' he countered, and her spirits plunged again.

'I'm looking forward to meeting her,' she lied again. 'I've seen a couple of her films and I thought she was quite a good actress.'

'Tell her that and she'll be your friend for life!' he grinned. 'She's not so much an actress as a glamorous prop! And she's caught the public's imagination. Like Raquel Welch did. There's no doubt that having her in a film helps to sell it.'

'What she does, she does well, though,' Emma said.

His eyes glinted mischievously. 'I can agree with you there.'

'How long will she be staying at the villa?' Emma asked hurriedly.

'Until she gets bored. It could be anything from two days to two months.'

'What makes her bored?'

'Lack of male attention.'

'But *you'll* be there.'

'I may not want to be attentive once she's signed the contract!'

Emma gasped. 'How unscrupulous you make yourself sound!'

'I don't only sound it, my child. I *am*. Remember that.'

She had no need to wonder why he was warning her. Though she tried to hide her growing attraction to him, he was too used to women not to know how drawn she was to him. It was a sobering thought, and she was relieved when he paid their bill, and suggested they leave the hotel.

'I thought we'd dine at Mario's in town,' he said as they drove away. 'I hope you like Italian food?'

'I love it.' Her nose wrinkled at the pleasurable thought. 'I suppose if I were a true gourmet I'd never admit it, though. Isn't it sacrilegious to admit to liking anything but French cooking?'

'Only to a Frenchman,' Jake said. 'I'm afraid I'm not a worshipper at the shrine of Michelin! I've tasted superb food in many countries—even England!'

The restaurant was packed, but Jake was treated like an honoured guest. They were ushered past the waiting crowd in the overflowing bar to the pretty patio outside, which was covered by an awning that matched the blue checked cloths on the tables.

As he had predicted, the food was excellent, and as Emma appreciatively tucked into creamy fettuccini, followed by Escalope parmigiano, he looked on in wonderment.

'For a mini-sized girl, you have a maxi-sized appetite!' he remarked.

'Now you'll make me feel guilty when I order dessert!'

'I don't believe you'll have room for it?'

'Care to bet?'

'No.'

Emma drained her glass and Jake refilled it from the

wine bottle in the ice bucket at the side of the table.

'Would you like me to order another bottle?' he asked as he poured the remaining liquid into his own glass.

'I've had too much already,' she replied. 'I'm not much of a drinker. One more glass and I'd be under the table.'

He laughed. 'What vices do you have? You don't smoke, you hardly drink, and you're still a virgin. God! That's a daunting combination! You're almost too good to be true.'

Emma looked away from him, not sure if what he really meant was too dull to be true.

'A man should never be allowed to know everything about a woman,' she parried. 'Keep 'em guessing. Isn't that the name of the game?'

'I wouldn't know. I never play by the rules.'

'Strictly a nonconformist?'

He nodded. 'And I make a point of preaching what I practise! That way I even make converts!'

'I hope you're not expecting to convert *me*?'

He stared at her, then he took one of her small hands in his and held it lightly while he gazed into her face.

'Could I?' he asked, and then repeated softly, 'Would you, Emma?'

She felt herself blushing as awareness of his touch set her heart racing. How confident he looked sitting opposite her, tall and fair, his hair curled at the ends and ruffled at the back where it touched his collar.

'I'll get the bill,' he said before she could answer, and gently took his hand away.

They drove back in silence. The fine night streamed away on either side, with the summer breeze blowing her hair away from her face. She leaned back against the soft leather seat and closed her aching eyes. The next thing she knew they had come to a halt outside the door of the villa.

Emma blinked and yawned. 'I'm sorry about that,' she excused herself. 'Wearing my contact lenses all day made my eyes tired.'

'As long as I didn't bore you to sleep!' he smiled, and went round to the boot to take out her shopping. He did not bother to put the car away; instead he accompanied her upstairs and put the boxes on her bed.

He stood hesitantly at the doorway and then came back into the room and pulled her into the crook of his arm.

'I enjoyed being with you, Emma. Thanks.'

With a sigh she rested her head against his chest. She knew she shouldn't, and that if she had even a modicum of sense, she would pull away from him. But oh, how dull it was to be sensible all the time! She remained where she was and he bent forward and raised her chin with his fingers, cupping her face in his hands as he gently pressed his lips on hers. His touch was soft, and she trembled with nerves. But her longing for him was too strong to be denied and she began to respond to him.

'I won't hurt you,' he whispered against her mouth. 'There's nothing to be afraid of.'

She felt the warmth of his breath and the rise and fall of his chest. How sure of himself he was, showing none of the nervousness she was feeling. If she were not so inexperienced she could pretend to be as nonchalant as he was. After all, he was only kissing her—hardly a momentous happening in anyone's book.

His hands moved down her back, drawing her body closer. She was aware of every muscle in his body pressing hard against her, and once again she trembled, a sharp movement that made him tighten his hold, as if he were afraid she would fall.

'You're like a will o' the wisp,' he murmured huskily, his face against her hair. 'If I let you go, you might blow away.'

As if to ensure she did not, he clasped her face between his hands again, his eyes looking deep into hers. Then he lowered his lids and his head came down until once again his lips were pressed on hers.

This time his kiss was firmer, and she responded with a passion that took him by surprise. He did not need to force her lips apart as he had done that day in the study, for they parted readily, her mouth opening beneath his. His lips probed gently as she stood on tiptoe to put her arms around his neck. His beard was soft against her face and felt like down, and she clasped him tightly and wound her fingers into the thick hair at the nape of his neck.

Abruptly Jake pulled away, doing so with obvious reluctance.

'That shouldn't have happened,' he said. The thickness of his voice told her he wanted her as much as she wanted him, though perhaps for different reasons. 'You're a very desirable young lady, Emma. That air of innocence brings out the worst in a man. I hadn't realised I'd find it so susceptible.'

'I'm glad you did,' she answered boldly, her cheeks scarlet as poppies.

'You wouldn't, if I hadn't stopped myself in time. I don't seduce children.'

'I'm not a child,' she said sharply, nervous with pent-up emotion. 'I wish you'd stop treating me as if I were.'

'As far as making love is concerned, you *are* a child.'

'That's a cruel thing to say! Didn't I arouse you?'

'You know damn well you did. But you're inexperienced and it would be all too easy for me to arouse *you*.'

'I wouldn't have gone to bed with you,' she said.

'Really?' His tone was so superior that she knew he did not believe her. 'If I'd gone on kissing you and touching you, you wouldn't have been able to stop yourself. Believe me, Emma, I know what I'm talking about.' His lids lowered, masking the expression in his eyes. 'Sex is no more than an enjoyable game for me, but it wouldn't be for you. You deserve something better for your first night of love. For a start, I suggest a ring on the third finger of your left hand.' He turned on his heels and walked towards the door, then faced her again. 'Wait for that, my child. You'll feel happier.'

As the door closed behind him, Emma dissolved into tears. How dared he treat her in such a condescending way? She was twenty-one and old enough to make her own sexual decisions without the help of Jake Sanders—lover first class! He acted as if he were an old roué and she just out of a convent. The fact that she believed in the institution of marriage and had no intention of sleeping with any man beforehand was beside the point. She did not need *him* to tell her not to do so. If she wanted to go to bed with him that was up to her. Of all the infuriating men to fall in love with. . . .

She sank back on to the cushions as the full implication of those words hit her. She couldn't be in love with Jake Sanders! But she was. Yet she was not even sure if she liked him. Not that it mattered, since he would never reciprocate her feelings and had made it perfectly clear that marriage was the last thing on his mind. The best thing for her to do was to go back home. At the thought of it, her heart sank. She could not leave him. Not yet. Hadn't he told her he found himself susceptible to her? At least that was something, and she was always on hand. . . . She gave a half laugh. Usually it was the woman who played hard to get, but in her case it was the reverse.

CHAPTER SIX

In the morning, heavy-eyed and listless, she prepared breakfast, then deliberately remained in the kitchen, allowing Carmen to take it out to Jake. If he wanted to see her, let him come to her.

And that was just what he did; looking unusually serious without a twinkle in his eyes.

'I hope we can still be friends after last night?' he asked gently. 'I didn't mean to upset you, Emma. I only did what I thought was best in the circumstances.'

'Don't give it another thought,' she said airily. 'It was just that the wine went to my head. I'm relieved you had the sense not to take me seriously.'

'Good.' He went on regarding her. 'If I didn't like you so much, I'd never have left your room. But I meant what I said last night. You deserve a man who can love you wholeheartedly, not someone who merely wants an affair.'

'*Would* you have an affair with me?' Emma asked so lightly that she made it sound like a joke.

'Any time,' he chuckled. 'Just let me know when you're ready to toss your principles to the wind.'

'I'd rather toss you!'

'That's my girl,' he said admiringly. 'You know, Emma, for a pint-size filly, you've got a gallon-size tongue!'

Still chuckling, he sauntered out, and Emma restrained an urge to kick him. How blind he was! Didn't he know she was fast losing all the restraints of her old-fashioned upbringing? But it was a good thing he *didn't* know. Loving a man like Jake was painful enough, but to make that love a reality would make it doubly hard for her to forget him when she left here. Her vacillation disturbed her. One moment she was determined to fight for him; the next, she was conceding that no woman would ever get him to the altar.

'Emma!'

Jake's unexpected return to the kitchen made her jump nervously. 'What's wrong?' she demanded.

'Nothing. I just wondered if you'd worked out what to get for the dinner party on Friday?'

'Yes, I have.' She did not tell him she had finished it during her sleepless hours last night. 'Would you like to see it?'

'I thought we agreed you were to use your own judgment?'

'I wasn't sure if you'd changed your mind.'

'I rarely change my mind.'

Was he giving her a subtle warning? Resolutely she took his reply at face value. 'In that case, I'll go ahead as ordered.'

'If you need Carmen to help you, tell her.'

'I'm a professional cook, Jake,' Emma admonished. 'I can prepare dinner for ten as easily as for two.'

'But you look so fragile I——' abruptly his lips came together. 'How about joining me for a meal on the patio tonight?'

'Aren't you taking a risk?' she asked with a smile. 'I might force my attentions on you and have to be carted off in a straitjacket when you refuse me!'

'I'll keep a sedative handy to slip into your drink if you become too hot to handle!'

Emma made herself give a tinkling laugh, though it died as soon as he left the kitchen. She knew she was playing with fire, but since she was already burned. . . .

With a sense of relief she set off for Paguera, shopping

list on the seat next to her, and it was nearly noon before she returned to the villa. As soon as she had put away the vegetables and fruit she had bought, she ran up to her room to change. If she didn't have a swim before starting on her cooking, she'd end up a greasy puddle on the kitchen floor.

Opening the dressing-table drawer, she took out one of the bikinis she had purchased yesterday, but after glancing out of the window and seeing no sign of Jake by the pool, she put it back and took out her old black costume. She would save her new outfit for a more suitable occasion.

For nearly half an hour she swam undisturbed except for the dragonflies that hovered over the water, their gossamer wings lightly touching the surface as they too cooled themselves from the heat of the day.

When she returned to the kitchen she set about doing the night's dinner, and also preparing the food for the party. Carmen had told her that *gaspacho* was one of Jake's favourites, and she had decided to serve this as the first course. Apart from a small amount of olive oil, it was mainly tomatoes, onions, peppers and cucumbers: nothing to which calorie-conscious ladies could object. By the time the vegetables were marinating, it was time for Jake's lunch, and she popped a mushroom quiche in the oven—which she had made a few days earlier—and hastily prepared a green salad. Thank heavens for the deep freeze! She had baked several quiches with different fillings and frozen them, giving herself snack meals to hand that only required a short time in the oven before serving.

To her surprise, Jake came into the kitchen after lunch to compliment her on the pastry, and Emma hugged his words to her as if they were nuggets of gold.

'We won't want anything better for lunches when the family are here,' he told her. 'My brother and his wife both watch their weight, so they certainly won't want to eat two large meals a day. And fruit will be fine for desserts,' he added.

'They'll get fed up with pastry every day,' she protested.

'It's so light, you hardly know it's there.' He gave her a humorous look. 'Rather like you!'

She turned back to the stove so that he could not see the look of pleasure that flooded her face, and all afternoon she read different meanings into the remark, one minute taking it as a compliment, and the next as a light-hearted attempt at flirtation.

That evening Emma did not put on one of her new dresses, not wishing Jake to think she was dressing to attract him. Instead, she settled for a floral cotton in hues of green and blue, that emphasised her tan. But she paid careful attention to her hair, brushing it vigorously to make it shine, and wearing it loose.

Over dinner Jake continued to charm her, first by remarking on her outfit and then complimenting her for the excellent meal, which he had eaten with relish.

'I'm amazed that this is your first professional job. You don't cook like an amateur,' he remarked as he sipped his brandy.

'Even if I kiss like one!' she replied before she had a chance to stop herself. Darn it! Now he would think she was flirting with him.

'I thought we were going to forget about last night,' he said whimsically.

Emma looked across at him as he puffed his cheroot. Relaxing against the white cushions of the wicker lounging chair, with his red cotton shirt open at the neck to show the blond hairs on his bronzed chest, he looked so devastating that she longed to rush over and hold him. How could she possibly forget last night, when what she ached for was a repetition? Deliberately she sought for something to say.

'What made you grow a beard?'

He looked surprised. 'Do you always change the subject so abruptly?'

'I thought that was what you wanted?'

'I thought it's what we both wanted,' he argued gently.

'So answer my question, then.'

'I grew it to hide a scar. I had an accident last winter skiing at St Moritz, and my chin was badly cut. I suppose I could have plastic surgery, but I thought I'd give this a try first. I've always wanted to grow one. Don't you like it?'

'Very much. It was a new experience being kissed by a man with a beard.' She bit her lip and stopped. 'There I go again! I think you'll have to give me that sedative!'

Jake laughed. But before he could say anything, the telephone rang, and he went to answer it.

He spoke for several minutes, and then came back with an irritated look on his face.

'Damn it! That was one of my dinner guests. Her husband has gout and can't make it.' He looked at Emma. 'You don't play bridge by any chance, do you?'

'I'm afraid not.'

'That's a shame. We're playing tomorrow after dinner and you could have made up one of the tables. When I'm the host, I prefer to sit out.'

Emma could not suppress a smile. 'I imagined you'd be dancing after dinner.'

'As my youngest guest is sixty-five, I think you can discount that idea! As a matter of fact, I play bridge most evenings.'

'You do?'

Her surprise made him give her an intent look. 'Where did you think I went?' One look at her face was sufficient answer, and he wagged his finger at her. 'You shouldn't be so quick to judge me, little girl. I don't go in for the swinging life here—through necessity, I might add, not choice.'

'What do you mean?'

'Well, most of the English residents are retired, and lead a quiet life. Bridge is almost a must if you want any kind of social life—that is apart from the endless rounds of boring cocktail parties, which I happily forgo.'

Emma was still not sure she believed him, and he was quick to sense it.

'You're as bad as Celia,' he chuckled. 'She also refuses to believe I lead a perfectly chaste existence down here. That's why she likes coming down to check up on me and see if she can spot the competition. So far she's been disappointed.' Jake puffed out a cloud of smoke, and through the haze gave Emma a searching look. 'I don't think she'll try to get her claws into *you*. She knows you're not my type.'

Emma's spirits plummeted. How honest Jake was! How hurtful without realising it.

'I suppose you like sexy-looking blondes?' she said coolly.

'Isn't that the sort most men prefer? That's why the producers of my next film are so anxious to have Celia play the female lead.'

'You make it sound as though she might refuse.'

'That's *exactly* what she might do. For the past year Celia's been hankering after dramatic roles, and we're having the devil's own job persuading her to make this picture.'

'Wouldn't she do it for *you*?' Emma asked boldly.

Jake hesitated, his mouth firming. 'Probably. We've been very good friends, as you know.'

Emma felt the colour rise in her face, and was angry with herself. No wonder Jake called her an innocent!

'Aren't you still?' she murmured.

'You're very curious about my affairs,' he countered. 'Are you going home to write a series about me for one of the scandal sheets?'

'However did you guess?' Emma hid her hurt at his remark. 'That's the only reason I've stayed here, as a matter of fact—so I could write all about your sex life.'

'Without first-hand experience?'

'Definitely without first-hand experience.'

His teeth gleamed white in his bronzed face. 'My affair with Celia has been over for a long while. As you know, I don't stay with any girl too long, in case they start seeing wedding rings and hearing bells.'

'But your name's still linked with hers,' Emma could not help saying.

'Only for the sake of this new film. It's good publicity—that's partly the reason she's coming here. But knowing Celia, she'll take the opportunity to try to make more of it. She's too dumb to know that when something's over, it's over.'

'Maybe she's still in love with you.'

'Our relationship had nothing to do with love. But I suppose I'll have to make sure she's kept happy while she's here. If she pulls out, the money men might follow suit.'

Emma swallowed hard. She did not need to ask what Jake meant by keeping Celia happy.

'I'm sure you won't find it a hardship,' she said aloud.

'I wish *I* were so sure. There's nothing more dead than dead passion.'

Emma remained silent. Regardless of his last comment, Jake would do his best to fan the embers—if that was the only way he could get Celia Manners in his film. It seemed a pretty low thing to do, but then he was ambitious and ruthless enough for it not to trouble his conscience.

'I think it might be a good idea if we turned in,' said Jake, rising. 'You've got a busy day ahead of you tomorrow. It will be a dress-rehearsal for next week.'

'I know.' Accepting his comment as a desire to end their discussion, she made her way upstairs, conscious of Jake following close behind.

He stopped at the door of her room, but only to bid her a polite goodnight, before walking to his own at the far end of the corridor. The wall lights threw his shadow behind him, and she watched it, knowing it would disappear when he switched off the electricity. If only she could make him disappear as easily from her mind! It would be a relief when his family arrived next week, and they were no longer alone. But more especially it would do her good to see him with Celia Manners. Once she saw them together it would rid her of any silly ideas she entertained of Jake finding *her* desirable.

The following day was hectic, and flew by with barely a moment to relax. Carmen brought her daughter with her in the morning, and they set about laying the table and arranging the flowers that had been delivered from Paguera. Jake kept out of the way, working down by the pool, and Emma had no occasion to speak to him.

The guests were arriving at eight, and by seven everything was ready. Carmen's husband Rafael was attending to the drinks, and he busied himself at the wicker bar on the terrace, wiping the glasses and sprinkling the champagne goblets with sugar, ready for the cocktails.

Everything went smoothly, and by ten o'clock Emma was exhausted and ready for bed. She went up to her room as soon as coffee and home-made petits fours had been served, and fell asleep almost immediately, in spite of the soft voices that floated up from the garden as the guests settled down for their bridge games.

It was not until the following morning that she saw

Jake again, when he came into the kitchen to talk to her. It was getting to be part of his morning routine.

'It was a great dinner, Emma. Even though all the ladies were dieting, not one of them could resist your milles-feuilles.'

'There's still one left,' she smiled. 'I saved it for you, for today.'

'Not for me,' he said firmly, patting his flat stomach.

'Frightened of getting fat?' she mocked, looking at his lithe figure, clad in the same frayed shorts as when he had met her at the airport.

'I prefer to call it practising self-control!' He came over to the Magimix and dipped his finger into the mixture, nodding approvingly as he licked it off. 'This tastes good enough to eat already. What is it?'

'Spicy apple cake. It's served warm with whipped cream.'

He groaned. 'I'm beginning to wish you'd gone back to England on the first plane!'

So am I, Emma thought soberly, knowing that each day here added to her storehouse of memories, and would make it that much more difficult to forget this man.

Yet despite knowing the heartache in store for her, she basked in the compliments he heaped upon her culinary prowess. It was amazing how lighthearted happiness could make one feel. Apart from preparing the meals, she whipped up cakes and biscuits and ice cream, then prepared several different soups and pâtés without the slightest feeling of exhaustion, and placed them all in the freezer. She felt as if she were floating on air. If the only way she could get to this man's heart was through his stomach, she would do her best to ensure that every dish she set before him was fit for a king.

Yet he made no mention of taking her to Formentor, as he had promised, and she wondered whether he regretted having made it, or had forgotten. Either way, it did nothing for her ego, though she knew that the less time she spent alone with him the better.

On Monday, before leaving for the airport to collect his family, he took her by surprise by apologising for not taking her to Formentor.

'I had to make some last-minute alterations to the script, and I wanted to finish it while I was alone,' he explained. 'Celia's contract—if she signs it—gives her script approval—though as she's never read anything in her life other than her own publicity—I'm damned if I can see her understanding what *I've* written.'

'I'm sure you'll be able to help her,' Emma said coolly.

'I intend to do my best.'

Emma's disgust was so strong that it was an effort to hide it. Yet she knew she was being naïve. He and Celia had obviously been lovers, so what did it matter to him if he resumed the affair? Refusing to give it any more thought, she set about preparing lunch. That's why I'm here, she reminded herself, and vowed not to forget it.

While there were guests at the villa, Carmen's daughter was coming in every day to help out, although Emma had offered her own services.

'You're here only to cook,' Jake had told her adamantly. 'Cleaning up after spoiled women was *not* part of the bargain. In any case, if you don't devote your full time to the meals, your standard might drop.'

The latter explanation robbed her of the desire to thank him. So he had been thinking more about his own stomach than giving her extra work!

Despite knowing this, she was pleased she did not have to do general work around the villa. At least she would not be required to clean up after Jake's girl-friend, even though she would have to feed her.

It was noon when she heard him return from the airport, and shyly she made her way out to the hall. He spotted her instantly and made the introductions.

His brother, David, was quite unlike him, being dark, and starting to lose his hair at the crown. He was stockily built with a slight paunch, and had a brisk voice that sounded as if he were used to giving orders and having them obeyed.

His red-haired wife looked as though she could stand up to him. She took Emma's hand and gave her a warm, friendly smile. Pamela Sanders was an attractive girl of about twenty-eight, rather on the plump side, with long slim legs offsetting her well-rounded hips. Her voice was firm as she directed her husband and Jake as they carried the luggage upstairs, and Emma had the impression that David Sanders might well be the boss in the office, but his wife was very much so at home!

Nanny Lee looked like a martinet, with her wispy grey hair scraped back under her stiffly starched navy cap. Her nose was long and pointed, and her mouth thin and pursed, as if she found everything about the house and its inhabitants disagreeable.

'I do hope baby's room doesn't get the sun,' she stated disapprovingly as she walked up the stairs, carrying the gurgling chubby baby, his plump little hands pulling at her silver-framed glasses.

'None of the rooms get the sun, Nanny,' Jake answered patiently from the top of the landing.

She snorted. 'Your parents never took *you* abroad when you were young. Frinton was good enough for them. I don't hold with the heat for young children.'

'There are a lot of things you don't hold with, Nanny, that I do,' Pamela Sanders reproved her gently, but Emma could see that she held her temper with difficulty. Obviously this was the end of a long line of complaints in a similar vein.

As Emma turned to go back to the kitchen, Jake called her, and she swung round to look at him.

'I'll expect you to join us for lunch,' he said.

'I'd rather not. Carmen and Maria are here and they'll——'

'They won't care *where* you eat,' he cut in. 'And they're both intelligent enough to know that you'll be more at home dining with my family than with them.'

Accepting the logic of this, Emma did not argue, and found herself warming to Jake for his open friendliness. He might be a Casanova and male chauvinist, but he was certainly no snob.

Lunch was eaten al fresco, with the family tucking into cold chicken and a variety of salads. Toby's high chair was placed in the shadiest corner, and by the time Nanny Lee had eaten, her attitude had noticeably softened.

'You have a lovely place here, Mr Jake. The house and gardens are beautiful—and so tidy.'

Jake chuckled. 'Just because I was untidy in the nursery, there's no reason to suppose I wouldn't change when I grew up!'

Nanny turned to Emma and gave an indulgent smile. 'He was one of the naughtiest little boys I ever looked after; but when he smiled, you could forgive him anything.'

'And now he's a naughty big boy,' Pamela chipped in with a grin. 'And women are still forgiving him when he smiles!'

In the afternoon the baby was put down to rest, and Pam—she much preferred the abbreviated version of her name—suggested Emma accompany her to the beach.

'Nanny's going to follow later with Toby, so we can get to know each other while the men go off and discuss business. David's dying to, aren't you, darling?' She threw a loving glance at her husband, who was sipping his coffee.

'That's exactly what I intended doing,' he agreed. 'There are a few things I must clear up with Jake.'

Emma went up to change, and for the first time put on one of her new bikinis with its matching skirt. She looked at herself in the mirror, not sure if it was too brief. There appeared to be a rather large expanse of skin between the revealing top of her bikini and the tiny pants, but after a moment's contemplation, she decided she was being silly. Her figure was excellent and it was childish to want to hide it.

Slipping on her sandals, she went down to join Pam, who had also changed, and they walked slowly through the pine trees to the beach.

'I'll get David to bring some chairs down and leave them here,' his wife decided. 'That's what we usually do.' She turned and looked at Emma admiringly as she slipped off her sarong-style skirt and walked to the water's edge. 'I'd never have guessed you looked like *that* underneath the tent you wore this morning! How on earth do you stay so slim?'

'Luck, I guess. No matter what I eat, I don't put on weight.'

'I wish I didn't.' Pam looked ruefully at her plump figure. 'I put on stones when I was expecting Toby, and I haven't had the willpower to lose it all. That's what being married does for you. David likes me this way, so I've no incentive.' She sat down on the shore and allowed a gentle wave to break over her. 'Now if I'd married Jake, he'd have *made* me diet.'

Emma looked at her curiously. 'Were you and Jake engaged?'

'Not really. But we've known each other since childhood, and Jake and I were always paired off.'

'But you preferred David in the end?' Emma asked.

'I did the sensible thing. I was frightened of marrying Jake.

'Frightened?'

'Would *you* feel safe married to such a gorgeous hunk of manhood?'

'Probably not,' Emma agreed, and was surprised when Pam contradicted what she had said a moment earlier, by adding:

'One day I think Jake *will* settle down and make a fantastic husband. But it has to be in his own time, without any prodding from the girl.'

'I bet lots of them do more than merely prod!' Emma said matter-of-factly.

'Who can blame them?' Pam eyed her. 'Don't tell me *you* haven't fallen for him? I've never known a woman who hasn't.'

'I have a boy-friend in England,' Emma replied carefully, not wanting to give this sharp-eyed girl a chance to guess her feelings.

'As if that matters,' Pam snorted. 'It wouldn't make any difference if you had a husband! If Jake set out to win you, you wouldn't stand a chance!'

'*You* didn't succumb.'

'I did in the beginning, and it took me years before I realised I wasn't the type to keep him. But luckily David suits me very well. He's solid and dependable, and allows me my own way—most of the time. With my red hair, that's a recipe for happiness!'

'So it's natural,' Emma smiled.

'Everything about Pam is natural,' a voice behind them said, and they turned to see the two men. David smiled affectionately at his wife. 'I'll race you to the raft,' he told her, and swiftly plunged into the sea with Pam rapidly chasing after him.

'How about joining them?' Jake asked, his eyes taking

in Emma's near-naked figure, and she jumped up quickly and ran into the water.

Panting, she reached the raft before him, and he watched as she hauled herself up.

'You look almost as good from behind as you do in front,' he remarked as he clambered up after her.

She heard Pam giggle. 'You never say that to me, David.'

'I leave the prose to Jake,' her husband grunted. 'He's the writer in the family.'

They lay basking in the sunshine until Pam spotted Nanny on the beach with Toby, and then she and David swam back.

'They're nice,' Emma remarked, with the wistfulness of an only child.

'Pam's got a sharp tongue at times,' said Jake, 'but she's the right wife for my brother.'

'But not for you?' Emma blurted out before she could stop herself.

Jake leaned on one elbow and looked down at her, his blue eyes locking with hers. '*If* I wanted a wife, you'd do very nicely. You've got a good mind; you're an excellent cook, and although you're tiny, you're very appealingly packaged!' Bending forward, he kissed the tip of her nose, and then let his lips travel gently downwards, kissing both corners of her mouth before coming to rest there.

Emma felt the warmth of his breath, and tasted the salt of the sea on his lips as he slowly and sensuously urged her lips apart. She moved closer and stroked his thick hair. As the intensity of his kiss deepened, he pressed the weight of his body down upon her, his hands moving restlessly on her back as he clasped her to him. As she felt the rough tangle of his hairs on her breasts, her desire increased, and she arched upwards and pressed her mouth against his ear.

'I love you,' she whispered.

He pulled back as sharply as if he had been stung.

'Don't say that!'

Dismayed, she stared at him. Moments before his face had been filled with desire; now it was cold and distant.

'Don't say things like that,' he repeated. 'Not even as a joke. I'm not the marrying kind, and I'm definitely not the man for you.'

'What makes you so sure?' she asked huskily.

He did not answer immediately, but sat gazing blankly out to sea.

'I've never been in love,' he said finally. 'I don't even know if I'm capable of it.'

'Yet you write about love. How can you, if you've never experienced it?'

He gave a sardonic laugh. 'I've never experienced rape, but I write about that too! But as you so aptly pointed out, my books are concerned with lust, not love, and *that* I can write about from knowledge.'

Flushing, Emma sat up, and Jake turned his head and let his eyes move over her face. Then he reached for her hand and squeezed it. 'Don't lose your heart to me, Emma, I'm not worth it. My advice to you is to go back home to your young man and live happily ever after.'

'I wish you'd stop treating me like a child!' Emma drew her hand away sharply. 'I'm perfectly capable of making my own decisions. If you imagine I'm reading anything into a few kisses, you're quite wrong. I find you attractive, but I'm certainly not in love with you.'

'Then why did you say you were?'

'I got carried away by the romantic setting,' she lied. 'You have to admit it could hardly be bettered. Blue sea, lonely raft and a golden-haired Adonis. I mean, it's pure Hollywood.'

Before he could reply, she dived into the water and swam furiously back to the beach.

Fortunately Pam and her husband were too preoccupied playing with the baby to take any notice of her, and Emma lay down on her towel, her mind seething. What a fool she had been to blurt out that she loved Jake! Luckily she had managed to convince him she hadn't meant it, but if she lost her head again and said it, it might not be so easy to make him believe her.

Blast Jake Sanders! Why couldn't he have been old and ugly, or sent her back to England as soon as he realised he had engaged the wrong person? Emma stood up and shook the sand from her towel.

'I'm going to make tea,' she announced.

'I'll come with you,' said Pam. 'I'm all sticky from the sand.' She turned to her husband. 'I'll leave you to finish making that fort. Perhaps when you've done it, you'll allow Toby to have his bucket and spade back!'

The two girls walked up towards the house in companionable silence, and while Pam went to wash, Emma made tea.

By the time she wheeled the trolley on to the patio, both men had returned and Pam had changed.

'Shall I pour, or will you?' Emma asked her.

'The pleasure can be all yours,' Pam replied, cutting herself a large slice of almond cake. 'I intend to do as little as possible this holiday.' She whirled round and pointed a finger at Jake. 'And don't dare say, but you always do!'

Jake chuckled. 'I wouldn't dream of it, so long as you don't expect Emma to clear up after you, when the staff go home. It's not part of her duties.'

'I assume kissing her on the raft *is*!' Pam retorted, though there was no malice in her voice.

Emma went fiery red. 'Jake was merely keeping in practice until Miss Manners arrives,' she put in with a smile that belied her true feelings.

'Ah,' David's voice broke in, 'our lovely little sex-kitten.'

'Sex-cat, you mean,' his wife said. 'There's nothing playful about dear Celia.'

'Don't be bitchy,' warned Jake. 'It doesn't suit you.'

His sister-in-law went over and kissed him on the cheek. 'I'm sorry, Jake, but you know I can't stand her.'

'Well, you'd better, for all our sakes,' her husband butted in. 'Jake's getting a percentage on this new film as well, and if it's as big a hit as the last. . . .'

'Don't say any more!' Pam grinned. 'I'll be sweetness itself to Miss Kittycat.' She yawned and moved to the door. 'What time is dinner? I think I'd like to have a rest first.'

'Would eight-thirty be too late?' Emma asked. 'I'm going in now to start preparing it.'

'Suits me,' Pam smiled.

'And me,' said David, rising and putting his arm around his wife's waist. 'I think I'll join you, darling.'

Emma went to leave with them, but Jake signalled her to wait. Warily she watched him, wishing she were not so conscious of the taut muscles that ran along his broad shoulders and down the sides of his strong, firm legs.

'You're annoyed with me, aren't you?' he asked as soon as they were alone.

'You're not still going on about what happened on the raft?' she exclaimed in astonishment. 'I told you before, I enjoy being kissed by you. *You* have the touch of the master—even if I haven't the touch of your mistress!'

His eyes narrowed. 'I think you'd make an excellent mistress—with a few more lessons.'

'Changing your mind about me, Jake?' she demanded pertly.

'No. Appealing though you are, I've never enjoyed

picking flowers fresh from the garden. I prefer them already cut.'

'And handled,' she replied, walking out nonchalantly before he had a chance to answer her.

But in the kitchen her air of coolness disappeared and she banged the saucepans about to give vent to her feelings. However childish, it had been enjoyable to have the last word! But oh, what a swine Jake was!

CHAPTER SEVEN

THE following day Emma received two letters, one from her grandmother, giving all the village gossip, and the other from Peter, telling her he had booked into a hotel in Paguera for his holiday. 'I hope your boss will allow you to have extra time off,' he wrote, 'so that we can be together.'

Emma was dismayed at the prospect of his visit, knowing she could never marry Peter now. Jake had spoiled her for most men, possibly all, for a long time to come. It was a frightening thought and could mean years of loneliness.

She was grateful for the extra work that new guests brought, for it kept her too busy to think. On a few occasions they went out for dinner, and insisted she join them, which was a bittersweet pleasure, since it meant seeing Jake at his polished best. Even Nanny Lee turned out to be pleasanter than she had first supposed. Underneath the crusty exterior she was as soft as a marshmallow, though she was firm with the baby, and kept him to a strict routine, which he appeared to enjoy. He was very little trouble, the description 'fat and happy' being well applicable in his case.

But fat was not happy for Pam, and she found it difficult to resist the cakes which Emma served at teatime.

'I wish you wouldn't make them,' she protested one afternoon. 'I die a little bit each time your apple cake and chocolate gateau appear.'

'Why should we suffer because you've got no will-power?' David interjected as he bit into a slice of Sachertorte. 'You keep up the good work, Emma, and don't mind Pam.' He turned to his wife. 'We'll both go to a health farm when we get home, so stop worrying about your figure.' He gave her bottom a slap. 'Anyway, I like you this way—there's something for me to get hold of! Why you women think that all men like skinny figures beats me.'

Pam gave a resigned sigh and sliced a piece of the sticky cake for herself. 'I surrender willingly—like the lovely Celia!'

David glanced over to where Jake, sitting on the far side of the pool, was intently studying a pile of manuscripts. 'She's coming tomorrow, isn't she?'

'As if you didn't know!' Pam grinned. 'And since it's our last night of freedom from her, how about all of us going to a night club?'

'Suits me,' said David, and called over to his brother, 'Fancy a night out, Jake?'

Jake lifted his head and nodded. His glance strayed to Emma, and she had the strong impression he had not been as oblivious of the whole conversation as the rest of his family supposed.

'You'll join us, won't you, Emma?' he asked.

She wanted to refuse, but knew that if she did, she might give herself away. She had only one choice: to play it coolly, as if being with Jake left her quite unperturbed.

'Why not?' she replied airily. 'How could I pass up a chance of dancing with the great Drake Janess!'

'How indeed!' he retorted, and lowered his head to his papers again.

Later that evening, Emma debated which of her dresses to wear, finally choosing a rose silk chiffon with a pleated skirt. The wide belt with its diamanté clasp showed off her small waist, and the shoestring straps of the bodice alluring revealed her high, firm breasts. Her hair had been bleached by the sun, and was streaked with auburn highlights, while her tan had brought freckles out on the bridge of her nose. She applied more make-up than usual, as if it could mask her feelings, using black mascara instead of brown to lengthen and darken her thick lashes, and choosing a lipstick in a sizzling pink that toned perfectly with her dress.

She stared at her reflection before going downstairs, but though she knew she looked unusually lovely, she also knew that in Jake's life there had been a surfeit of equally pretty females. And Celia Manners was a beauty; there was no denying it.

When she reached the downstairs hall, everyone was waiting for her, and though Pam and David commented how charming she looked, Jake said nothing, and silently took his place behind the wheel of the car, leaving the two girls to sit in the back.

'I like you with more make-up,' Pam whispered. 'Jake's eyes nearly popped out when you walked down the stairs!'

Emma was sure the other girl was exaggerating, yet could not help being pleased. At least Jake must have shown *some* sign of approval, for Pam to have noticed it.

Within the hour they drew up outside Tito's in the heart of Palma. The doorman, who instantly recognised Jake, took the keys from him to park the car in the crowded street. The pavements were thronged with tourists, who overspilled into the road, and they had to fight their way through to the foyer.

As they walked towards their table, Emma was conscious of the way all the women, young and old, turned admiringly to Jake, just as they had on the day he had waited for her in Palma when she had gone shopping. But he appeared equally oblivious to them, which only added to his attraction. No man had the right to be so magnificently built and so good-looking, Emma thought despairingly. It was heaping gift upon gift. With a faint sigh, she dropped her eyes away from his thick blond hair which, even in the subdued lamplight, glowed like gold.

The nightclub, set out in the open air, was enormous, but its size in no way detracted from its beauty. It was tiered in terraces, as if in a garden, and each table was softly lit by shaded lamps.

They sat listening to the Latin-American music, and soon its hypnotic rhythm persuaded David to take to the floor with Pam.

'Shall we join them?' Jake asked Emma, and without waiting for her nod, drew her to her feet.

He clasped her close as they swayed to the rhumba, and at his touch Emma felt the usual tell-tale desire for him that his closeness always aroused. But Jake did not appear to notice, and swept her around the floor as the music changed to a fox trot. She barely reached his shoulder, and yet she felt comfortable in his arms, as if she belonged there, and their steps were perfectly matched as they gave themselves up to the strident beat.

'Why are you trembling?' he asked suddenly. 'Is it fear or desire?'

Anger coursed through her, giving her the impetus to answer with sarcasm. 'Desire, of course. I'm mad about you—and I adore your books.'

'*That* I don't believe!' His eyes glinted sharply. 'But I'm prepared to believe you want *me*—for other reasons.'

'Lust,' she answered pertly. 'Women feel it as well as men.'

Another couple bumped into them, and Jake muttered under his breath, and swung her away. But the floor was packed, and they were now pressed even closer together.

'Rather than be *pushed* around, I'd prefer to sit down,' he said, and led her back to join his brother and sister-in-law.

Hardly were they seated when two middle-aged women, both plump and blonde, came over to the table and beamed down at Jake.

'Aren't you Drake Janess, the author?' one of them gushed, staring at him from green-painted eyes. 'I said to my friend, I'd recognise your face anywhere. We're such fans of yours, Drake. We loved your last book—much better than Harold Robbins—and we saw the film three times.' She rattled on, barely stopping for breath. 'I wonder if you'd autograph these cards for us? This one's for my friend. I'm Joan and she's May.'

She handed him two postcards, and Jake gave her a brilliant smile and scribbled a message on them with the pen she had at the ready.

Murmuring profuse thanks, they walked off, turning to look admiringly at him until they reached their table at the far side of the dance floor.

'Does that happen often?' David asked.

'Ever since the film came out, and my affair with Celia was spread all over the gossip columns.'

'The price of success,' Pam commented. 'Your mother was horrified when she saw that picture of you in the *Sun* with Celia, topless.'

Jake looked irritated, then half smiled. 'I don't believe you, sweet sister-in-law. The parents never read that paper!'

'One of the maids showed it to her,' Pam asserted. 'The

only thing that pleased her was that you'd grown a beard, so she hoped most of her friends wouldn't recognise you.'

'Mother probably thinks I grew it as a disguise to please her,' Jake said sourly. 'Only *my* parents would be ashamed of a son who's made his fortune honestly.'

Once more Emma sympathised with Jake. She might not care for his books either, or like his free style of living; but he did not seduce innocent girls—as she knew—and could not understand why his parents weren't proud of his success.

'Why did you change your name?' she asked the question that had long been on her mind. 'And where did you find it?'

His good humour returned at her question.

'It's an anagram of Jake Sanders. If you did crossword puzzles you'd have spotted it immediately.'

'I'm hopeless at puzzles,' she admitted.

'But you understand *me*.'

'You're as easy to read as your books!'

'Which you despise.'

Aghast, she stared at him. 'I—I . . . That doesn't mean I despise *you*. All I meant was——'

'I know what you meant,' he overrode her stammering apology. 'Forget it, Emma, I was only teasing you.'

They did not leave Tito's until three, having waited to see the famous singer who was heading the cabaret bill. On the way home, Pam insisted on sitting with David, saying the champagne had made her feel sleepy and she wanted a shoulder to lie on.

Whether this was a ruse to ensure that Emma sat next to Jake, she did not know, but she suspected the older girl of matchmaking tactics. It was obvious Pam disliked Celia, and for some reason seemed to think Jake might be more than passingly attracted to Emma. If only *she* were as confident!

'You look very serious,' Jake interrupted her musing. 'Anything worrying you?'

'I was thinking of tomorrow's meals,' she fibbed.

'Now that it's past twelve the princess turns back into Cinderella again,' he teased, 'and all thoughts are in the kitchen!'

'That's what I'm being paid for,' she stated flatly. 'I don't want to let you down.'

'I have no fear of that. You're the one mistake that I'm pleased I made!' He turned to eye her. 'Though I'm sure Celia would prefer you if you *did* have a moustache!'

'Will she be arriving for lunch?'

'I doubt it. There's sure to be local reporters at the airport. Her press agent will have seen to that.'

'I wouldn't have thought the Majorcan papers were worth bothering with, from a publicity point of view.'

'They aren't. But what they print is often picked up by Associated Press, and that goes all over the world. It happened on her last visit here. I'm surprised you didn't see it in the gossip columns: Actress arrives for secret rendezvous with author.' He gave a snort. 'Some secret!'

'How did you first meet her?' Emma asked.

'On the set of the film.'

'Does she live in America now?'

'Yes, she's a tax exile. That's what usually comes with fame and fortune.'

He seemed in such a receptive mood that Emma wanted to go on questioning him, but unfortunately they drew up outside the front door of the villa. He swivelled round to look at his brother, who was fast asleep, with Pam's head resting on his shoulder.

'Four years ago he couldn't keep his hands off her,' he said softly. 'But now look at him! That's what marriage does to you.'

David straightened up and yawned. 'I wasn't sleeping,

old chap. But making love in the back of a car is only fun when you're single.'

'With some people making love anywhere is only fun when you're single!' Pam said merrily. 'Come on, Casanova, let's see if walking up the stairs will get your adrenalin working again!'

They disappeared inside, and Emma waited while Jake put the car away.

'Thank you for a lovely evening,' she said demurely.

'And please may I get down,' he answered, equally so. 'You sound just like a little girl at the dinner table. You don't have to be so formal.'

'How else should I express myself?'

'Like this,' he replied, and swiftly pulled her into his arms. 'You're so lovely, Emma. I've been wanting to do this all evening.'

His hand caressed her lightly, though his lips plundered the moist sweetness of her mouth. She tried not to respond, but it was hopeless, and her own lips emulated the movements of his. Instantly she felt his body stiffen and he pulled her hips tight against him, making no attempt to hide the way she was arousing him. Only then did Emma feel sickened by his response, knowing he saw her as no better than all the other willing girls to whom he had made careless, unthinking love.

With a sharp wrench she pulled free of him. 'Now *you're* the one who's being formal,' she said shakily. 'Always kiss your date goodnight, and tell her she's lovely.'

One golden-blond eyebrow rose. 'Do you think I'm pretending?'

'What else? But it's second nature to you. Miss Manners arrives tomorrow and you'll be doing the same with her.'

'Only for business reasons. Unlike you, it won't mean anything.'

Emma longed to hit him. 'I don't mean anything to

you either. No woman does. You're too scared of commitment.'

'Perhaps you could make me change my mind,' he ventured softly.

'For how long—till the next pretty girl comes on the scene?'

'You're more than pretty, Emma.' Jake had an odd expression on his face, as if he were seeing and assessing her for the first time. 'You're intelligent, and humorous and honest. It's a rare combination. I'd enjoy teaching you about love.'

'I'm sure,' Emma retorted. 'But could you also *love* me, apart from merely wanting me?'

The warmth evaporated from his face, leaving it a hard, cold mask. So must he look at the end of an affair, Emma thought bleakly, and forced herself to speak lightly, as if her question to him had only been a joke.

'Let's just be friends, Jake. It's better this way.'

'Don't you want an answer to your question?' he demanded.

'I thought it was an obvious one.'

'No,' he said slowly. 'In fact it's more complicated than I realised. Let me give you an answer when Celia's signed her new contract. For the next few weeks I have to dance attendance on her. But after that, things could be different.'

'So could I,' said Emma. 'My emotions don't stay the same, Jake. I'm a changeable girl—youth and all that.'

'I'll take a chance on it.'

With a shrug, she sidestepped him and went to her room. She longed for him to come after her, but was thankful that he didn't. How cleverly he had left her dangling in mid-air, convinced—despite her denials—that he had her hooked and could land her any time he chose. Through her inexperience she had acted like a teenager with her first love affair. Instead of playing hard to get, she had made herself easily available. No wonder he believed he could keep her in cold storage until it suited him to defrost her when Celia left!

His affair with the star might be over, but he was willing to pretend otherwise until she had signed to appear in his new film. Business before pleasure—that was Jake's axiom in life. And it would always be that way.

CHAPTER EIGHT

EMMA fell into an uneasy slumber, from which she forced herself to appear cheerful when she went downstairs in the morning. Luckily the weather did not match her mood. Each day was unfailingly glorious. The sun shone as brightly as newly minted gold from a sky as clear and blue as a field of cornflowers. The only variation came in the late afternoon, when occasional wisps of fine cloud, like puffs of cottonwool, drifted across the sky.

Pam wandered into the kitchen after breakfast and sat with her for most of the morning.

'I love watching other people cook,' she remarked as Emma chopped some mushrooms. 'Especially when they know what they're doing. It's fascinating how all these rather unappetising ingredients,' she pointed to the raw meat, garlic and onions, 'are going to end up as delicious sauté of veal Marengo!'

Emma laughed. 'Don't you like cooking?'

'Not much. If I did, David and I would be even fatter than we are.' Pam rose and busied herself with the percolator. 'Let's have some coffee. You've been on the go for the past two hours and it's time for a break.'

Gratefully Emma nodded, and watched as Pam set three cups on the tray, adding the bubbling percolator and marched towards the patio.

'What about a cup for Jake?' Emma asked.

'You're right,' said Pam. 'I haven't heard him drive off to the airport yet.' Setting the tray down, she reached for another cup and saucer. 'You two didn't have a quarrel last night, did you? Jake looked a bit strained this morning, and snapped my head off when I told him so. It could be the natural effects of Celia's arrival, but I've a feeling that you're the cause.'

'Your feelings are wrong,' Emma said emphatically. 'Jake wouldn't be affected by any quarrel with *me*.'

'Don't be so sure. He's never looked at any of the other. . . .' Pam stopped short and reddened.

'Any of the other cooks in quite the same way?' Emma finished for her. 'I rather had the impression he'd grown tired of having lady chefs who saw *him* as their dish of the day!'

'Only because he knew Celia was coming and he didn't want to upset her. But until now, he's always chosen attractive girls to cook for him. Attractive and—and——'

'Girls who knew the score?'

'Sort of,' Pam admitted, encouraged by Emma's seeming coolness. 'Usually they're content to love him and leave him. After all, three months with Jake is better than no Jake at all! Unfortunately, the last one was not so obliging and took the whole thing too seriously.'

This was not quite the same story Emma had heard from Carmen. According to the maid, the cook had been fired for using too much pepper. Still, maybe it amounted to the same reason. Too hot to handle—in more ways than one!

'Jake told David he was definitely going to engage a man this time,' Pam added, 'so we had quite a surprise when we came here and found *you*.'

Emma turned quickly to the oven to hide her expression. 'I must look at the casserole,' she muttered. 'I don't want to give Miss Manners a burnt offering her first day here.'

'She might not be as forgiving as Jake!'

'He told you about that disaster?'

Pam giggled. 'And also how you squirted him with the siphon. If he forgave you that, he must——'

'I'm off to the airport now,' said Jake from the doorway, and Pam abruptly stopped speaking. 'David wants to go into Palma, so he's coming with me.'

'In that case I'll join you,' Pam said. 'I fancy browsing around the shops. I'll only be a few minutes changing. Can you wait?'

Jake nodded and sat down while Pam went to her room. 'I'll have a cup of that coffee, if it's still hot.' He helped himself when Emma made no move to pour it. 'Am I getting the silent treatment?'

'No, sir. I'm merely making sure Miss Manners is given no cause for complaint.'

He gave a wry smile. 'God himself couldn't guarantee that! You'd think, with Celia's looks, she'd have no need to be jealous of any woman.'

'But she knows what a roving eye you have,' Emma said sweetly. 'So it's doubly important for me to keep my place—sir.'

'I can't see you doing it for long.'

'Really? Do you think you're so irresistible, then?'

He grinned. 'Aren't I?' he said, leering at her.

'Not to me,' she replied and slapped him hard across the face.

The cup and saucer he was holding fell to the ground and broke, but other than that, Jake gave no sign of being surprised or annoyed by her action. It was almost as if it had never happened.

'Now that's what's known as a shattering experience!' he said quietly.

Mortified by her behaviour, Emma bent to pick up the broken china. 'I'm sorry, Jake. That was childish of me.'

'You *are* a child. A Victorian one, with Victorian ideas about the way men and women behave.'

She straightened and put the pieces of china on the tray. 'You're right. I'm afraid the only thing we have in common is that we both wear contact lenses.'

'But yours are still rose-tinted. Change them, Emma, and see things the way they are.'

'What a clever comment,' she said brightly. 'But then, being a writer, you're never at a loss for the telling phrase, are you?'

'Thanks for calling me a writer,' he replied. 'On the last occasion we discussed my profession, you described me as a literary hack.'

'I don't remember using the word *literary*.'

'Now you're hitting below the belt!'

'That's certainly one place you couldn't be described as a hack!'

His eyes glittered and the mockery left his face. 'Be careful, Emma,' he warned. 'Don't try me too far.'

'I don't want to try you at all!'

Without a word, Jake turned on his heels and went out.

Trembling, Emma sank down on a chair. If she had purposely set out to make Jake dislike her, she could not have done a better job. Still, perhaps it was better this way. At least he would no longer be interested in seducing her, once he was free of Celia. The thought should have made her happy, but inexplicably it had the opposite effect. The emotions Jake aroused in her were playing havoc with all her firmly held beliefs about marriage and virginity, and she knew how easily he could have overcome them. But then love made you an easy prey to desire. She lowered her head in her hands and wished she had listened to her grandparents and never come here.

With a sigh she straightened. 'Stop thinking this way,' she said aloud. 'You're being defeatist. You had to fall in love some time, and what better lesson than to fall for one of the world's biggest wolves? At least you'll be inoculated for life!'

Trying to believe what she was saying, she went upstairs to don a swimsuit, then spent half an hour in the pool, trying to think what she would do when she eventually left here. Not marry Peter, that was for sure. Loving Jake might bring her misery, but it had also increased her self-confidence. Why, she was one of the few females—possibly the only one—whom he had fancied but not had. It was an exhilarating thought, and she concentrated on it.

She was back in the kitchen, putting the finishing touches to a bombe à l'orange, when Pam rushed in, laden with parcels.

'Could you be an angel and make us some tea, Emma. We're parched!'

'Has Miss Manners arrived?' asked Emma.

'With five suitcases.'

'You'll need to buy another one as well, to take back your purchases!'

'I know. But shoes and bags are super here—and much cheaper than in London.'

With a wave Pam was gone, and Emma quickly laid the trolley and wheeled it out. Her heart was pounding, but her cool manner gave no evidence of it as she poured the tea and cut the cake.

Jake was engrossed in conversation with Celia, and did not look up, and the girl was the first to do so. Even though Emma was prepared to find her beautiful, she had been secretly hoping that her screen image had been flattering: but if anything, it did not do Celia justice. In real life she was even lovelier. Her corn-coloured hair was thick and shiny and cut with a fringe in a straight bob, falling just below her ears. She rose and came over to the trolley: five foot seven inches of glorious femininity: full bust, narrow hips, and legs that seemed to go on for ever. The clinging silk of her dress, the bodice stretched tautly over her bra-less breasts, showed every curve, and when she paused to reach out for a cup of tea, Emma felt completely insignificant.

'You must be Emma,' she said in a husky, well-modulated voice. 'I've been hearing all about you.' Exquisite rosebud lips formed a smile, but the large grey-green eyes with their black-rimmed irises were cold and sharp, like two chips of ice.

'I hope you only heard good things,' Emma answered conventionally.

'Of course—don't all good things come in little packages?' The look that accompanied this remark made it clear that Celia only considered big to be beautiful!

'Milk or lemon, Miss Manners?' Emma enquired.

'Lemon, please, and do call me Celia. I hear you're on a first-name basis with everyone else, and I hate being formal with the staff.'

'How very democratic,' Pam chipped in. 'I suppose that's what living in America does for you!'

Celia ignored the sarcasm. 'I was the same before I went—wasn't I, Jake?' She looked to him for confirmation.

'You certainly were, my sweet,' he answered laconically.

Celia's tapering fingers, with their long, blood-red nails, picked up a small slice of cake. 'Jake tells me you're a marvellous cook.'

Emma bit back a desire to giggle. It seemed as if quite a bit of their conversation had centred around her. It could hardly have endeared her to Celia.

'You'll be able to judge for yourself this evening,' she murmured. 'I hope you have a good appetite?'

'I do when I'm not filming. But even a few extra pounds shows up before the camera.' She regarded Pam, who was helping herself to a large piece of cake. 'You're lucky you don't have a slim figure to worry about, darling.'

'Luck has nothing to do with my figure!' Pam answered goodnaturedly. 'But over-eating has!'

'At least you're tall, so you don't look too bad. It's short girls who have to be careful.' Celia appraised Emma. 'I suppose you're always counting the calories?'

'When she gets to ten thousand a day she stops!' Jake intervened with a chuckle. 'You wouldn't believe what this little one can put away.'

'More tea, anyone?' Emma asked meekly, noticing Celia's lips tightening as Jake came to her defence.

'Not for me,' said Celia, turning to Jake. 'Darling, could you come up and have a go at undoing the lock of one of my cases? It seems to be jammed.'

Jake stood up and with a nod, followed Celia into the house.

'I was wondering how she was going to get him upstairs,' Pam commented.

'You don't need an excuse to get *me* upstairs,' David interceded with a leer.

'In that case I'm off to see to dinner.' Emma gathered the remaining cups and wheeled the trolley out, feeling herself to be a spare wheel in a car that already had four tyres.

Unsure about setting a place for herself at the dinner table, she instructed Carmen to only lay for four. Nanny rarely ate dinner with the family, and Emma decided that she wouldn't do so either. Her presence might annoy Celia, and no doubt after the reconciliation which was taking place at this moment, Jake would not wish to do anything to displease her.

But she was wrong, for shortly after eight he came in search of her, his mouth set in a tight line of annoyance.

'Why have you only laid for four?' he demanded.

'Because I'm not a guest. And now that Miss Manners is here. . . .'

'When I want something changed I'll tell you!'

'I don't think it's a good idea for me to eat with you. And frankly I'd feel more comfortable if I didn't.'

'Well, I wouldn't.' He ran his hand through his hair, ruffling the front so that a thick blond strand fell forward. 'You seem to enjoy the role of Cinderella, but I refuse to let you play it.'

'Prince Charming to the rescue,' she sniffed.

'If you like. But please stop casting Celia in the role of the Ugly Sister!'

'Never an Ugly Sister,' Pam commented, coming into the kitchen with a champagne glass in her hand. 'I think the Wicked Witch is far more her part!'

Jake rounded on her angrily. 'How many times do I have to tell you that it's important not to upset her?'

'She can't hear me,' Pam protested. 'But you must admit she's a prize bitch when she wants to be. "How lucky, Pam, that you don't have a slim figure to worry about," she mimicked Celia's voice expertly, and even Jake could not help a smile. 'I had a wonderful retort ready, but for your sake I held my tongue.'

'Not an easy thing for you to do,' he smiled, 'and I appreciate it.' He turned back to Emma. 'Now, go up and change, will you? You're eating with us—and no argument.'

Dinner went off better than could be expected, considering Celia's initial surprise when Emma joined them. The star had floated into the room on a cloud of Joy and silk chiffon, her creamy shoulders bare, except for an emerald scarf lightly draped around her swan-like neck. Although Emma had changed into one of her new dresses, a white broderie anglaise, she knew she could not compete against Celia—few women could—and wondered for the umpteenth time how Jake could remain immune to such beauty. Except that he wasn't immune. He desired Celia—regardless of what he said—and had no problem in satiating that need.

'How clever of you to remember I only drink Bollinger,' Celia cooed at him as he handed her a goblet of champagne.

'How could I forget?' he said suavely, and gave her one of his intent looks.

They made a striking couple: both tall and blond—though Jake's colouring was natural—and both exuding that raw sexuality that would make heads turn wherever they went. If he were not a writer, Emma decided, he could easily become a film star. It was a wonder he wasn't both. A man with his determination to be a success could probably follow more than one career.

'Did you manage to get the lock of Celia's case undone?' Pam asked her brother-in-law innocently.

Jake looked at her expressionless. 'Just about. I never was much of a handyman, though—that was always David's speciality, if I remember rightly. Another time I'll let *him* take over.'

Pam grinned, and raised her glass to him.

Celia looked from one to the other in bemusement, and Emma hid a smile. Beautiful the girl might be, and bitchy too, but brainy she wasn't.

'I'm hungry,' Celia said petulantly. 'It's nearly nine, and I hate eating late.'

'Dinner's ready any time you want it,' Emma said smoothly.

'Then what are we waiting for?' Jake replied, and gallantly extended his arm to the girl beside him.

During dinner, Emma felt very much left out. It was all very well for Jake to insist she dine with them, but meanwhile no one bothered to speak to her. Celia monopolised him completely, discussing the new film and the many friends they had in common, while Pam, who had had too much champagne, was making amorous overtures to her husband.

Emma excused herself as soon as coffee was served, and was pleased that her departure went unremarked. The sight of Jake taking Celia in his arms to dance would have been more than she could bear, knowing of the hour he had already spent alone in the girl's room.

The soft strains of Andy Williams wafted up to her from the terrace as she lay in bed, and she padded over and closed her window. Better to suffer heatstroke than to hear romantic lyrics being crooned into another girl's ears.

What a strange man Jake was! He did not mind using any woman to suit his purpose. After all, hadn't he used her until Celia reappeared on the scene? Once he'd recovered from the shock of discovering he had hired the wrong person, he had felt duty bound to continue his old egotistical habit and make her succumb to his charms. He had probably hoped to seduce her quickly and enjoy her favours until his mistress arrived.

She frowned in the dark. In all fairness, he had not tried that hard. Had he done so, she was by no means certain what her reaction would have been. It was easy to moralise when temptation was not put in your way. But since she had met Jake, her whole persona had been turned upside down, and she hoped that Peter's arrival would change her back to her usual self. But somehow she doubted it.

During the next week, Jake and Celia went out to dinner a few times with David and Pam, and Emma was able to catch up with her correspondence. For the remainder of the evenings they ate at the villa and usually danced until the early hours, although she always retired early, as on the first occasion, unwilling to put Jake in the invidious position of having to dance with her out of politeness.

In the day, Celia spent much of her time reading Jake's script, and from the look of contentment on his face, it appeared things were going well. Annoyingly Celia managed to acquire a tan without the slightest hint of redness—unusual in someone so fair. She rarely ventured into the pool—and then only at the shallow end. Getting her hair untidy was almost a phobia with her, and it always looked as shiny and immaculate as the day she had arrived, even after hours of lying in the hot sunshine. Unlike lesser mortals, she never perspired. A truly golden goddess!

The following Monday morning Jake appeared in the kitchen. It was the first time he had seen Emma alone since Celia's arrival, but if she hoped for a personal conversation, she was very much disappointed.

'I have two more guests arriving this afternoon,' he said. 'Celia's agreed to do the film, and the producer's flying over with our lawyer to sign the contract.'

'You must be delighted,' she murmured.

'I am.' He stifled a yawn, and she wondered nastily if he was having sleepless nights in Celia's bed.

'Will your guests be staying the night?' she asked.

'No, only for dinner. But I'd like you to lay on something special.'

Emma nibbled worriedly at her lip. 'I wish you'd given me more notice. Nanny's gone into Palma with Pam and I promised to look after the baby.'

'Don't worry about Toby. David and I will keep our eyes on him. He's a good kid, and no bother.'

'Because Nanny plays with him all the time. But he's at the age when he's into everything.'

'Stuff him with chocolate and he won't budge!'

'Except to be sick.'

'You women make such a fuss about looking after children,' Jake said superciliously. 'I can assure you he won't be any bother to us.'

Emma remembered these words when, later that afternoon, David came tearing into the kitchen, his face scarlet with concern.

'Come quickly—it's Toby—I can't get him out of Celia's hair!'

Wondering if he had suffered a brainstorm, Emma hurried out after him.

Where sun and water had failed to ruffle the girl's sleek coiffure, Toby had succeeded! The blonde tresses stood up in chocolate-covered tufts as the little boy's chubby hands tugged at her hair, and he chuckled gleefully as Celia attempted to pull away from him.

'Get this brat off me!' Celia screamed in fury.

Emma stifled a laugh and looked at Jake and David, who were doing all they could to unwind the baby's fingers from the blonde hair. But nothing would dislodge them. Toby had found a new game to play and he would not let go.

'For God's sake, Emma,' Jake grated, 'don't just stand there!'

Taking pity on him—though he deserved none—she knelt down beside Toby and dangled her own long hair temptingly in front of him. Delighted at new pastures, he transferred his sticky fingers from Celia's hair, and beamed at them all.

David breathed a sigh of relief. 'That was quick thinking, Emma.' He turned to Celia, who was biting back tears of rage as she inspected herself in a mirror. 'It's only chocolate, old girl. It'll wash out easily enough.'

'And then what do I do?' Celia snapped. 'I'm hopeless with my hair—that's why I have a comb-out every day in Paguera. If you can't keep your child under control, you should make sure you have someone around who can!'

'I really am sorry,' he said again. 'I only gave him the chocolate to keep him happy.'

'It certainly did that!' said Emma with a smile, as she put the gurgling infant down again.

'I'm glad you find it amusing,' Celia said frostily, and frantically attempted to brush her hair, which only succeeded in making the melted chocolate spread. 'There must be a whole bar of Dairy Milk on me!' she wailed.

'We could try getting Toby to lick it off!' David grinned.

Celia looked as if she had reached boiling point, and Emma determined to cool her down.

'Why not let me have a go at setting it?' she asked. 'I manage my own pretty well.'

'I wouldn't exactly call you Vidal Sassoon,' came the ungrateful reply. 'But I'll accept the offer.' Peevishly Celia led the way to her room.

Emma soon understood why Celia hated getting her hair wet. When washed it went into a tight unbecoming frizz, and it was only by exerting considerable pressure with the brush that she managed to straighten it to some semblance of its former glory.

'It looks better than it did before you started,' Celia muttered. 'But not much.'

'I never said I was an expert,' Emma pointed out. 'But at least you don't look like a bar of chocolate cream!'

They heard voices in the hall below, and Celia darted

out of the bedroom and rushed down to greet the two men who were standing there with Jake.

'And how's our golden-haired beauty?' the plumper of the two asked.

David chuckled, and when the others looked puzzled, he amusingly described Toby's misdemeanor. Making a superhuman effort, Celia forced a smile to her lips and joined in the laughter—indicating that she wasn't such a bad actress after all!

Emma took the gurgling infant from his father, and left them to their business discussion. Jake's eyes as they met hers gleamed with humour, and as she passed, he said softly:

'I've eaten all my words, Emma. In future I'll listen to your advice and leave *you* holding the baby! You're obviously a little mother at heart.'

Hurt that he could even make an apology wounding, Emma smiled coolly as she swept past him and took Toby upstairs. After cleaning him up, she tucked him into his cot for his afternoon nap, and then returned to finish her dinner preparations.

She remained in the kitchen for the rest of the afternoon, busying herself unnecessarily, and keeping an occasional eye on the baby, who woke up looking angelic after his sleep, and seemed quite content to sit in his high chair on the small patio outside the kitchen, banging a wooden spoon on the tray in front of him, and munching on a piece of apple.

When Pam and Nanny eventually returned, Emma was almost sorry to hand him over, and her errant thoughts wandered to a future when she was married and looking after her own child. Somehow he was as blond and blue-eyed as Jake, which just showed how stupid she was.

'I wish I'd been here to see Celia's hair,' Pam almost choked with laughter when Emma told her what had happened. 'I've been wanting to dip my own hands into it for the past week too!'

'It's a good thing you weren't here,' Emma scolded. 'Jake might have murdered you.'

Pam had the grace to look ashamed. 'Well, it's understandable, I suppose. Having Celia in his new film is very important to him. I'll be extra nice to her tonight, though I'm sure Jake's already smoothed her over—if you know what I mean.'

Emma did, only too well, and was so soured by the picture invoked that she was quite unable to join the group for dinner. Not that anyone missed her. Jake was preoccupied with his producer and lawyer, and Pam and David were charm personified to Celia, who basked in their attention like a cat in sunshine.

Lying sleepless in bed, Emma seriously debated whether she could go on staying here. Despise Jake though she did, she still found herself wanting him, and knew it would be all too easy to give in to him if he should ever change his mind about her. Not that this seemed likely. His interest in her since Celia's arrival had been teasing and mildly affectionate, and the girl would no doubt stay until September, when she herself would be leaving.

In the morning her depression lifted, helped by a letter from Peter, who gave her his time of arrival on Thursday, and hoped she could meet him at the airport.

When she saw Jake after breakfast, she asked if it would be in order to use the car that particular evening.

'Peter's plane gets in at eight,' she explained, noticing a flicker of annoyance pass over his face. 'I'll prepare a buffet supper for you, so you won't need to go out.'

'I wasn't thinking about that—we'll eat out anyway. But I'd forgotten your boy-friend was arriving so soon.' He gave her a searching look. 'Looking forward to seeing him?'

Emma shrugged and ignored the question. 'I hope things went well for you yesterday?' she asked instead.

'Helped by your excellent meal, they certainly did. The contract's signed and sealed and Celia is fully committed. Thank heavens I can now act naturally with her.'

'No one would have guessed you weren't.'

Jake's blue eyes were speculative as he regarded her. 'A love affair is like a game, Emma. It's only fun while you enjoy it. After that, it's tedious. That's how it's been with Celia these last few months.'

'But you had no scruples pretending otherwise?'

He shrugged. 'We never had more between us than a purely physical relationship; and she's not hard to fancy!' He saw Emma's look of derision and his mouth tightened. 'I don't expect you to understand my actions. You're too deeply embedded in middle-class morality.'

'I know you intend that as an insult,' she retorted, 'but I happen to take it as a compliment. What I consider virtues, you consider faults.'

'So as usual we end up disagreeing. On that cue, I'll depart! Incidentally, if your boy-friend's arriving on Thursday night, you might as well take the whole day off and pretty yourself up. Carmen can take lunch from the freezer.'

He went out, and Emma sighed deeply. It was strange how she and Jake quarrelled, when all the time she longed for him to take her in his arms and make love to her. Perhaps that was why. His nearness excited her body and sharpened her temper, making her long to hurt him as much as he was, unwittingly, hurting her. She forced herself to think of Peter, but it was difficult even to remember what he looked like, so filled was her mind with thick blond hair, vivid blue eyes, and a hard, muscular body with a soft, conquering mouth.

Only as she drove into Palma on Thursday did she

succeed in forgetting Jake. She knew it was only a temporary respite, but it did wonders for her mood, and she decided to take Pam's advice and have her hair restyled by a young Spanish hairdresser who, it seemed, was a miracle worker.

His salon was in one of the large hotels, and Emma, seeing the long line of women under the mass of dryers, almost lost heart and fled. Even as she turned to the door, a pretty young girl enveloped her in a pink smock and led her towards a slender, dark-eyed man who was standing behind an empty chair.

'A cancellation,' the girl explained to Emma, pushing her into the seat. 'Usually you have to book Señor Valdez ten days in advance.'

Hoping she would not regret fate's act, Emma started to explain what she wanted done to her hair, but the young man shook his head.

'I am the greatest stylist,' he announced. 'You let me cut my way. If you no like, you no pay.'

Hoping fervently she would pay and like, Emma gave up the argument, and closed her eyes as Señor Valdez set to with scissors.

An hour later she stared at her reflection in astonishment. Her long, heavy tresses had disappeared, and shiny brown fronds curled around her head like a feather cap, giving her pert face an elfin look. Her neck, free of its usual mass of hair, rose slender as a stem from her shoulders, making her feel swan-like and elegant. No longer was she a small girl, top-heavy in appearance, but a slender, petite one, graceful as a ballerina.

'I can't believe it!' she gasped.

'My new clients all say same,' the Spaniard replied. 'You pleased to pay?' he added with a smile.

'More than pleased, *señor*. I'm delighted!' She peered at herself again. 'Will it be an easy style for me to keep?'

'For you, yes. You have excellent hair. It stay put as soon as I cut it. Shake your head and see.'

Emma did as he ordered, delighted to see it did just that. The fourteen pounds she handed over was money well spent, if the admiring glances she received as she made her way through the crowded streets were anything to go by—and each time she passed a window and stopped to admire her reflection, she found it difficult to believe it was really herself.

Still with time to spare, she browsed around the smart shops in the Borne, which was the daytime centre of the town, admiring the expensive clothes in the chic boutiques and peering into the dusty antique shops for bargains. After passing the same boutique twice, to gaze longingly at the outfit in the window, she went inside, and in moments stood before the cheval mirror clad in soft green silk. The dress was lightly embroidered, with a deep V bodice scalloped across the shoulders and a scalloped skirt wrapped to one side. It showed every curve of her body as she moved, and with her gamin haircut gave her an air of sophistication she had never had before.

Only when the assistant discreetly whispered the price in her ear, and she quickly converted it from pesetas into pounds, did she have second thoughts. It was nearly a whole month's wages, but she was in a reckless, heady mood, induced by her changed appearance, and minutes later she came out of the shop, box in hand.

Although she reached the airport well before Peter's plane was due, looking at the computerised board, she could not see his flight listed. Going over to the enquiry desk, she was dismayed to learn that the plane was delayed because of a strike, and would not be arriving till midnight.

It was barely seven-thirty, but there was no point driving back to Paguera, and Emma wandered into the snack bar and ate a dried-up sandwich that reminded her of buffet sandwiches the world over! Afterwards she went over to the bookstall, and was amused to find a large display of Jake's book in Spanish and English. She bought a Ross MacDonald thriller and settled down on one of the plastic-covered benches to while away the hours as pleasantly as she could.

Several times she glanced at the information board, and at eleven-thirty was relieved to see that Peter's flight would soon be landing. But it was past midnight before he finally came through Customs, looking disgruntled and tired, though his face lit up when he spotted her.

'How marvellous of you to wait,' he greeted her with relief, kissing her lightly on the lips before standing back to examine her carefully. 'What have you done to yourself since you've been away? I can hardly believe it's you!'

'It isn't,' she teased. 'You've been kissing a stranger.'

'An extremely beautiful one,' he enthused. 'Your hair, and that tan—why, you're stunning!'

They walked together towards the exit, and he put his luggage in the Datsun's boot. It was only as Emma started up the motor that he stared at her with alarm. 'Hey, put on your glasses! Your looks may have changed, but I'm sure your eyesight hasn't.'

'I'm wearing contact lenses,' she assured him.

'I thought you found them uncomfortable?'

'Jake—Mr Sanders persuaded me to persevere. He wears his all the time.'

Peter digested this piece of information before enquiring after her job. 'From your letters, you seem to like it.'

'I do. They treat me more like a friend than an employee, and that's made a big difference. But I don't want to go on about myself. First tell me how my grandparents are.'

During the hour's drive she caught up on all the news

from home, and by the time they drew up outside the luxurious hotel entrance, Peter was starting to question her about Jake. Hurriedly Emma parked the car and led the way across the lobby to the reception desk, where he handed in his letter confirming his booking.

The clerk looked at it, then shook his head. 'I'm sorry, *señor*,' he said in fluent English, 'but we do not hold rooms after midnight. You should have telephoned to say you were delayed. I'm afraid we have given your room to another guest.'

Peter looked at the swarthy man with disbelief. 'But that's ridiculous! It's only one-thirty. Surely you know there's a strike on at London Airport? I'm not the only English guest who's arrived late today.'

'You are the only one who did not telephone. Our letter clearly states that you must arrive before twelve o'clock on Thursday night or the room will not be held.'

'Now look here,' Peter said belligerently, 'I've booked a room, and I shall wait in this lobby until you give me one!'

'As you please, *señor*. You will find the couches quite comfortable, but I do not think it would be wise to start undressing.'

Peter turned to Emma with a look of exasperation on his face. 'What the hell am I going to do?'

'There's only one thing you can do,' she replied. 'Come back to the villa. I'm sure Jake won't mind if you spend the night there, and in the morning you can look for another hotel.'

The clerk gave a smirk. 'You won't find it easy. This is the peak of our season, and all the hotels are full.'

'Thanks for nothing,' snapped Peter. 'I'll remember to tell my English friends how helpful you've been!'

Grabbing Peter's arm, Emma pulled him away from the desk. 'There's no point getting mad,' she murmured.

'All you'll do is aggravate yourself and amuse him. At least you'll have somewhere to sleep for tonight, and we'll start searching for another hotel in the morning.'

The villa was in darkness when Emma finally drew up outside it, and it was clear that everyone was in bed.

'What shall we do now?' Peter asked in a hoarse whisper as they stood in the hall, surrounded by his luggage.

'I'll put you in the staff quarters over the garage, and explain to Jake in the morning.'

'Are you sure he won't mind?'

'Of course not.'

'But I'm a stranger.'

'Do stop worrying,' Emma said irritably, remembering Peter's old-womanish ways now that the first flush of re-union was over. 'In any case, unless you want to sleep on the beach, there's nothing else you can do.'

Seeing the logic of her argument, Peter complied without further comment, and followed her up the back stairs behind the kitchen, to the well-furnished bedroom with its en-suite bathroom.

'They do the staff pretty well here,' he commented. 'I'm sure the Royal wouldn't have been more luxurious.'

'You wait until you've seen the main villa,' said Emma. 'It's straight out of Hollywood.'

'I like the idea of us being away from everyone else,' he commented, as he shut the door.

'What do you mean?'

'Come here and I'll show you.'

When she made no move, he crossed the floor and pulled her into his arms, kissing her hard on the lips. His were moist and soft and she could not help comparing them with Jake's firm, dry touch. But not wishing to hurt Peter, she bore it as long as she could, though she was unable to respond, and when she finally pulled away, he looked at her with longing.

'I've missed you terribly, Emma. I hope you've missed me?'

His plea sounded childish, though she knew it was only because she was used to Jake's nonchalant manner, and she felt even more guilty for comparing the two men. Peter was far less sophisticated, and though he often travelled abroad on business for his father, his horizons were narrow and his view of life as old-fashioned as her own. Fleetingly she wondered what experience he had had with women, and was surprised by the thought. Before meeting Jake, she had not given much consideration to sex, or worried about Peter's previous love-life, but now it was uppermost in her mind.

'I think it's done us good to be away from each other,' he continued. 'It's not only your appearance that's changed, but your character too. You seem more mature and womanly.'

'It's a wonder you ever bothered with me before,' she said dryly. 'I obviously needed a lot of improvement!'

Peter stared at her. Humour was not his strong suit, and he was not sure if she were joking. 'I was quite happy with you the way you were,' he said ponderously. 'You know that.'

'I was teasing,' she smiled. 'I think it's time we went to bed. You must be exhausted.'

'Not when I'm with you. The last thing I want to do is go to sleep.'

She deliberately misinterpreted his words. 'We can talk some more in the morning,' she replied, and edged towards the door.

'Talking wasn't what I had in mind,' he said playfully, and caught hold of her.

'Let me go!' She wriggled free of him. 'I may have matured in the past month—but not to that extent!'

The coldness in her voice dampened his ardour, and he

stepped back, looking crestfallen. 'I'm sorry, Emma. I don't know what came over me.'

'I do,' she said, opening the door. 'You've had a trying day and now you're having a *trying* night!'

He frowned, then seeing the pun, smiled. 'Okay, I can take the hint. I'll see you in the morning, then. What time's breakfast?'

'For you, any time. Have a lie-in—I'm sure you'll need it.'

Slipping out, she ran down the stairs and made her way up the main staircase to her room. It was only as she shut the door that she saw the glow of a cigar end. She gasped with fright, but before she could turn on the light, her arm was caught in a vice-like grip.

'Where the hell have you been until now?' Jake demanded, his voice low but full of fury. 'Do you know what time it is?'

Emma flicked on the light switch and ostentatiously looked at her watch. 'At the third stroke it will be three o'clock precisely! Have you been waiting up for me, sir?'

He glared at her, unamused. 'I couldn't sleep and went out for a stroll. When I saw the car wasn't in the garage, I thought you'd had an accident. The plane was due in at eight and I couldn't think what had happened to you. You can't have been *talking* to your boyfriend all this time.'

Emma hid her amazement. Jake sounded exactly like a jealous lover!

'Of course I haven't been talking,' she said. 'I've been in Peter's room making mad, passionate love. You and Celia don't have the copyright!'

'Have you been drinking?' he enquired sharply.

'Do I need to be drunk to make love?'

'If it's without a wedding ring—yes!'

'I can't see what business it is of yours if I decide to

stay out late. As long as I'm here during the day to do my job, you have no right to complain.'

'I'm sorry, Emma.' Jake pulled deeply at his cheroot. 'You're quite right, but the truth is, I've been worried as hell. You haven't driven at night here, and I honestly thought you'd had an accident.'

'You're forgiven,' Emma said instantly, and sat down on her bed to ease off her shoes. 'The reason I'm late is that Peter's plane was delayed by a strike, and when we arrived at the hotel they'd given his room away.' She hesitated, then said quickly, 'the only thing I could think of was to bring him back here.'

'You mean he's waiting downstairs?'

'No. I took the liberty of putting him in the bedroom over the garage. I didn't want to wake you up to ask you. I hope you don't mind?'

'Of course not. But will he manage to find a room in the morning?'

'Not according to the hotel receptionist—who was absolutely awful, by the way. But if the worst happens, Peter will go farther down the coast.'

'Why bother?' Jake said laconically. 'Let him stay here.'

'Here? The whole time?'

'Why not?'

'That's very nice of you, but——'

'But nothing,' Jake interrupted. 'Stop fussing, Emma, it annoys me. It's the obvious thing for your boy-friend to stay close at hand. It'll stop you disappearing, for one thing.'

'So there's a method in your madness,' she said calmly. 'I should have guessed. You're a cold-blooded man, Drake Janess.'

'Not too cold-blooded to notice your new hair-style,' Jake said softly, and carefully stubbing out his cheroot, tossed it through the window before coming over to the bed. 'I like it. It makes you look older and more sophisticated.'

She tilted her head in order to stare into his face. 'The way you like your women?'

'You could never be one of my women,' he said abruptly, and stepped away from her. 'I'll see you in the morning, Emma. Sleep well.'

Alone, finally, Emma started to undress. If she lived to be a hundred, she would never understand Jake. One moment he acted with a possessive concern quite out of keeping with their relationship, and the next he was almost cruel in his detachment, as if ashamed of having displayed any concern for her. But what did his concern mean? Did it cover a deeper emotion? She sighed heavily, knowing that it didn't. To him, life was a game to be played hard and fast, with no set rules. Even when he kissed her it was only part of the sport he excelled in—and held no significance for him.

Yet instead of his casual attitude repelling her, it drew her to him like a magnet, holding her fast and making it impossible for her to break free.

CHAPTER NINE

EMMA told Peter of Jake's invitation when he was having breakfast. He was delighted by the offer and, and as soon as he had changed into swimming trunks, she took him to the main patio and introduced him to Jake.

The two men appeared stiff with each other, which surprised Emma; she had anticipated Peter being formal, but could not fathom why Jake should suddenly become equally so. However, by the time she joined them for a pre-lunch swim, the atmosphere was more relaxed, thanks to Pam and David, who had sensed the tension and made a great effort to draw Peter out.

Yet again, Emma could not help comparing him unfavourably with Jake. It was not merely that he was pale as a meringue beside the other man's bronzed skin, but that he seemed so thin and gangling. Deliberately she made herself look at them both with detachment. It was not easy, but she managed it. No, she still felt the same. Peter, pale-skinned, with jerky movements, looked like a schoolboy beside Jake.

It was only when Celia appeared, having gone into Paguera to do some shopping, that Peter lost some of his boyishness and became more of a young buck. His eyes, which had slid admiringly up and down Emma's bikini-clad figure, were riveted to the blonde girl's near-naked body, and Celia, delighted at the sight of a new male, wiggled her bottom enticingly as she made her way down the mosaic-tiled steps of the pool.

'She's even better looking than on the films,' Peter murmured to Emma.

'I didn't know you'd ever seen her.'

'When you wrote that she was staying here, I went to see her last picture.'

Emma hid a smile. When she had suggested seeing it some months ago, he had adamantly refused to take her, and she had gone with a friend.

'Come in for a swim, Peter,' Celia called imperiously. 'I hate swimming alone.'

He stood up, flattered by her request, and walked over to the side. Arms poised above his head, he executed an immaculate dive. Her warning for him to move farther up the pool came too late for him to hear, and he sprayed her with water.

'You clumsy idiot!' Celia shouted. 'Look what you've done to my hair!'

'I'm terribly sorry,' he spluttered.

'So you should be. It's absolutely soaked!'

'It's only damp on the surface,' Emma called, aware of Peter's discomfiture. 'It will soon dry off.'

Muttering angrily, Celia clambered out of the pool and headed for the house. Peter, still in the water, watched her go before swimming over to the side.

'Is she always so bad-tempered?' he asked. 'She was barely wet, you know.'

'She has a phobia about her hair,' Emma soothed. 'You're not the first to upset her over it. Toby did too.'

'Toby?'

'Pam's little boy.' In an effort to lessen his embarrassment, Emma recounted the chocolate incident, mimicking Celia's behaviour and voice so accurately that David and Pam exploded with laughter. Even Jake could not hide his amusement, though he was careful to glance towards the house, lest Celia suddenly emerge.

'You're as good a mimic as you are a cook,' he remarked.

'And you're a sensational cook,' David added.

Peter glowed, almost as if the compliments were being directed at him instead of Emma. 'She's great at everything she does,' he said proudly.

'You're a better actress than Celia, too,' Pam grinned. 'You should have asked Jake to consider *you* for the part of his heroine!'

'I'd hate being a film star,' Emma replied. 'You never have any private life and you're always worrying over the way you look.'

'Not if you're an *actress*,' Pam insisted. 'Celia's only a clothes-horse.'

'I agree with Emma,' said Peter. 'Anyway, I wouldn't

want her to have that sort of career. At least cooking is a damned useful accomplishment, and one she can still do when we're married.'

Emma turned to him sharply, but Pam spoke first.

'I didn't know you two were engaged.'

'Nor did I,' said Jake, and looked at Emma. 'Why didn't you tell me when I was in your room last night?'

Emma went scarlet. 'Because you didn't stay long enough,' she answered sweetly, delighted by her quickness of mind. 'Jake was waiting for me when I left you,' she explained, to assuage the curious look on Peter's face. 'He was worried that I'd had an accident.'

'Are you always so concerned about your staff?' Peter asked Jake.

'Only the pretty ones.'

Emma gave a determined laugh and looked desperately towards Pam for help.

'How about lunch?' the older girl asked brightly. 'I'm starving.'

'So am I,' said David. 'Hurry up, Emma, before I take a bite out of *you*!'

Smiling at them gratefully, Emma made for the kitchen. She dared not let Jake see how furious she was, not while Peter was still around, but just wait till she was alone with him! What game was he playing at, anyway? And why did he want to make Peter jealous?

Her chance to ask him came sooner than she expected, for he sauntered into the kitchen as she was removing the *tarte à l'oignon* from the oven.

'I thought we'd have champagne to celebrate your betrothal,' he said, crossing to the small fridge where he kept the white wine.

'You know very well I'm not engaged!' she rounded on him furiously.

'That's all the more reason for celebrating,' he told her smoothly.

'Why did you tell Peter you were in my room last night?' she demanded, ignoring what he said. 'You knew damn well what he'd think.'

'That shows what a fool he is! If he doesn't know the sort of girl you are by now, he doesn't deserve to have you.'

'I'll be the judge of that.'

'You're not *much* of a judge.' Jake's expression was hard to define. 'Peter's not for you, Emma. He's a fool and a bore.'

'How dare you criticise him!' she blazed. 'You only met him this morning, so how can you know what he's like?'

'Because it's my business to assess people. And your boy-friend isn't hard to understand. He's narrow-minded and callow. If he loved you, he'd trust you.'

'What do you know about love?'

'Enough to try to stop you making an idiot of yourself. You're worth ten of him, Emma. If you're so set on marriage, I can introduce you to any number of men far more worthy of you.'

For an instant Emma was speechless. 'Well . . . thanks!' She finally found her voice. 'Would I have to pay you a commission?'

'Only to let me kiss the bride.'

'That's too high a price. I'd rather stick with Peter.'

'Never,' said Jake, his eyes glinting.

Emma's sense of humour began to wear thin. 'I'll thank you to keep your nose out of my private life!'

'But I want——'

What he wanted, Emma never discovered, for just then Carmen came in to wheel out the trolley, and Jake grabbed hold of a bottle of champagne and strode off.

'He in love with you,' Carmen hissed melodramatically. 'I listen outside door.'

'Then you misheard,' Emma replied. 'He just enjoys making mischief.'

'You wrong. I see Mr Sanders with many girls, but he no look at them like he look at you.'

'Sorry, Carmen.' Emma was still unconvinced. 'Mr Sanders doesn't like to lose a conquest, that's all. It's bad for his ego.'

The Spanish woman looked puzzled, her knowledge of English unable to cope. 'Me no understand.'

'That makes two of us,' said Emma with a faint sigh, and preceded Carmen on to the patio.

Jake was pouring the champagne, but apart from giving Emma a quick glance, he did not mention the engagement. But Emma was not deceived and knew, from the covert look he gave Peter, that beneath his suave exterior was an impish rogue waiting to surface when the opportunity was ripe.

Celia joined them half way through lunch. Her hair had dried without its smoothness being affected, and she was in a forgiving mood. She set about charming Peter, and Emma was happy to leave them discussing Celia's favourite subject—herself—and return to the kitchen to prepare the evening meal. She was tired from her extremely late night, and by the time she had finished making the pastry for the *boeuf en croûte*, she was in a daze of tiredness. Thoughts of Jake and Peter flitted through her head and, though she tried to maintain her anger against the man she worked for, she could not help thinking of the comments he had made about Peter.

A light kiss on her neck startled her, bringing her back into the present. 'Stop it, Jake!' she cried, and spun round sharply. But it was not Jake standing there.

'So I was right,' Peter said grimly. 'There is something going on between you two.'

'Don't be silly!'

'So why did you think it was *him* kissing your neck? He must have done it before.'

Emma felt her cheeks burn. 'He hasn't—at least, only in fun. You know what film people are like.'

'I'm beginning to find out,' Peter said angrily. 'Celia's been giving me a few facts about Jake Sanders, and I must say I'm surprised you stayed here. The man's an outright scoundrel. He has one woman after the other!'

'Why shouldn't he?' Emma demanded. 'He's not married. And wouldn't you like to do the same if you had the chance?'

'Certainly not!' Peter looked horrified at the suggestion. 'I may flirt a little, but I'd never—I'd never . . .'

'Yes, you would,' Emma said lightly. 'You had a damn good try last night.'

Peter went scarlet. The anger left him and embarrassment took over. 'Oh, heck!' He ran his hands through his sandy hair. 'You've changed, Emma. I thought this month had done you good, but now I'm not so sure. You were always such a quiet, sensible girl.'

'I've grown up,' Emma said flatly, 'and I can't revert to what I was. For the first time in my life I feel my real age—not like a prudish old maid.'

'I'd hardly call you prudish. I've been taking you out for a year and you've behaved quite normally.'

'It depends what your standards of normality are. Do you know, I've never had an erotic thought about you?'

Peter's mouth opened in surprise at her frankness. 'That . . . er . . . that sort of thing comes after marriage, not before.'

She looked at him with exasperation. 'This is 1982, not 1882. It isn't normal not to wonder about making love to someone. Haven't you ever wondered what *I'd* be like in bed?'

Peter's eyes met hers, then slid away. 'Certainly I have. But it's not the same for a woman.'

'Why? Women have feelings too.'

'I'm not saying they haven't. But it's up to the—to the man to bring those feelings out—when the woman is married to him.'

'Saying he can't?'

'Can't what?'

'Can't bring out those feelings. Saying the couple aren't sexually compatible.'

'If you're suggesting what I think you're suggesting,' Peter said softly, 'why did you rebuff me last night?'

It was an intelligent question and one which Emma could only answer truthfully. 'Because I don't love you—not enough to marry you, anyway. You know I've had lots of doubts about us, and being away from you has confirmed them.'

Once again Peter ran his hands through his hair. He looked hurt and young, and Emma wished this conversation was not taking place. What a rotten day it was turning out for him! But he had to know the truth, and it was better for him to learn it now, at the beginning of his holiday, rather than later.

'If you'd rather spend your holiday somewhere else,' she went on, 'I'm sure you could get into a hotel farther along the coast.'

'No,' he said quickly. 'I want to stay here. I'm not about to give you up without a fight, Emma. You've had your head turned by living among these people, and I still think you'll change once you've left them.'

'I won't change. And you shouldn't blame the fact that I have on Jake or his family.'

'Of course I blame them. They're rich and glamorous, and *you're* young and susceptible. But I assure you Jake Sanders—or anyone like him, would make you a lousy husband.'

'I agree with you.'

'Good.' Peter caught her in a bear-like hug and kissed her firmly on the mouth. Emma tried her best to respond, but still found his nearness embarrassing. Even the fumbling pressure of his hands on her body left her cold. Worse: it angered her. Yet remembering all the years she had known him, she was reluctant to hurt him by saying so, and though she pushed him away, she managed to keep a smile on her face.

'See?' Peter said smugly. 'You're still my girl.'

Happily he strode out, leaving Emma to ponder at the stupidity of men. No matter how hard he tried, Peter could never mean anything to her. Not now. Not since she had met Jake. He had awakened her—like the Sleeping Beauty, with a kiss—and nothing would ever be the same again.

That evening, when dinner was over they all sat around languidly listening to the stereo. They were far too replete to dance, however tempting the velvet strains of Ella Fitzgerald, and Celia relaxed on the hammock, her head resting on Jake's shoulder, occasionally nibbling his ear.

They made a beautiful couple, Emma thought with a pang of envy. It was difficult to believe Jake when he said he was tired of Celia. How could any man tire of her? Yet he did not look happy with that golden halo next to his face—if anything he seemed bored by her persistent amorous approaches. He probably only liked a woman as long as he was doing the chasing. Once he had them, he was anxious to be off to pastures new. Even knowing this could not change what Emma felt for him. Only time and absence would do that.

'Why don't we all go out for the day tomorrow?' Jake suggested, suddenly breaking the silence. 'I promised to take Emma to Formentor—so let's go there.'

'We can't all fit into one car,' David said practically.

'I know. So I'll take Celia, Emma and Peter with me, and give them the grand tour, and you and Pam can meet us at the hotel for lunch.' Jake looked at Emma. 'I'd like to leave by nine sharp, if that's all right with you. It's a difficult drive on the mountain roads, and there's a lot to see.'

'I'm not sure I want to go,' Emma replied, reluctant to spend a whole day in his company, even though other people would be with them. 'If I had a day here alone, I could do some baking and replenish the freezer. We're getting low on quiches.'

'No.' Jake was peremptory. 'You deserve a day off.'

'I agree,' Pam added. 'So why not take a change of clothes for the evening, and stay on and dance at the discotheque?'

'That's the best idea of the lot,' Celia put in, smiling languidly at Jake. 'We could even stay there for a couple of days. Emma and Peter could drive back with your brother.'

'I dislike staying in hotels,' said Jake. 'But if you're bored here and want to leave. . . .'

'Don't be obtuse, darling. I just wanted to get you to myself.'

Not waiting to hear any more, Emma rose quickly and said goodnight. To sit and listen to Celia and Jake sparring was more than she could bear.

CHAPTER TEN

As usual the sun shone in a cloudless blue sky when they set off for Formentor next morning. Emma had put her new green silk dress in the car's boot, and wore hip-hugging white jeans with an emerald striped top which drew a low wolf whistle of appreciation from Peter as he opened the car door for her.

Past Paguera they left the motorway, and Jake manoeuvred the car on the narrow mountain roads with relaxed expertise. Although it was only thirty miles to Formentor, the change in the scenery as they drove from one side of the island to the other was remarkable.

The windmill-dotted plains of the south soon gave way to rugged mountain terrain where, hidden among the folds of the hills, were small farming communities so primitive that the twentieth century seemed to have passed them by. The only traffic they passed as they twisted and turned along the ribbon-like road until they reached the village of Deya were donkey carts piled high with produce, and they were relieved to get out and stretch their legs and have a much-needed cold drink.

Nestling in the mountains, the village was surrounded by craggy peaks. Below were the old tiled roofs and terraces of oranges, lemons and gnarled olive trees clinging to the slopes.

'This place is much in vogue with artists and writers,' Jake remarked as they walked through the cobbled streets to a small café. 'I nearly bought a place here myself, but decided it was too far from the airport.'

'I can't understand a chap like you living in Majorca

when the whole world's your oyster,' Peter commented.

'I happen to think that Majorca's my pearl!' Jake smiled. 'I have enough of the bright lights for eight months of the year, and I come here to recharge my batteries.'

'If you worked and played at a slower pace they wouldn't be so run down!' Celia commented.

'Jake enjoys a fast pace,' said Emma. 'And his work is so mentally stimulating too.'

'How clever of you to recognise that fact,' Jake said smoothly. 'I knew you'd appreciate my books sooner or later.'

'Everyone appreciates them,' Celia intervened. 'You're a wonderful writer, Jake. That's why it's so easy to act in your films.'

'You don't act,' Jake grinned. 'You wiggle.'

'Don't be nasty,' Celia pouted, not taking his remark seriously. 'You've never had cause to complain of my talents!'

Emma stared resolutely at the scenery, wishing herself miles away.

'Why can't we stay at Formentor alone for a few days?' Celia went on. 'You've been so peculiar to me since I got here that——'

'Hush!' Jake interrupted, placing his fingers lightly upon her scarlet painted mouth. 'You don't want to shock Emma, do you?'

Celia giggled and darted a triumphant glance in Emma's direction, before focusing on Peter.

'Have I shocked *you*?' she questioned innocently.

'Of course not,' Peter said tactfully. 'Stars—like yourself—have different standards from the rest of us.'

'What an interesting comment.' Celia seemed genuinely to believe it. 'Not enough people realise how difficult it is to cope with one's talent.'

'I understand perfectly,' Peter replied. 'And you're an

excellent actress. You remind me of Marilyn Monroe when she was young.'

Emma hid a smile. It seemed a lawyer's tact could be useful at times.

'Marilyn Monroe?' Celia echoed, her eyes lighting up. 'How interesting you should say that. She's always been my idol. Why do I remind you of her? Is it my colouring or my voice?'

Peter gulped. 'I—er—well. . . .'

'Go on, Peter,' Jake said smoothly. 'Don't be shy.'

'It's your voice,' Peter said manfully. 'It has the same husky quality.'

Celia rose, cucumber-cool in green silk. 'Let's wander on ahead, Peter, and you can tell me more. You're obviously a very observant man.'

'What a good idea. I'll show Emma round the galleries,' Jake encouraged.

Throwing Emma a silent appeal for help as Celia linked her arm with his, Peter went off, leaving Emma alone with Jake.

'I think we can forget about Peter for a little while,' he remarked dryly. 'Celia will be happy to discuss herself non-stop.'

'Did you purposely try to annoy her?'

'Of course not,' he protested. 'I only do that with you!'

She ignored his comment. 'I think it was mean of you to land Peter with Celia.'

'He rather landed himself. Anyway, I'm sure he won't find it a hardship.'

'*You* seem to, otherwise why did you manoeuvre this situation?'

'Don't you know?' Jake rose and pulled her up with him, then set off at a brisk pace, walking in the other direction from Peter and Celia. 'Don't you know?' he repeated angrily. 'You're not *that* shortsighted, are you?'

'You mean that now Celia's signed on the dotted line you can continue trying to seduce me?'

'Seduction isn't what I have in mind,' he said grimly. 'If it were, I could have done that weeks ago.'

She reddened, knowing it to be the truth. 'You're the most insufferably conceited man I know!'

'I prefer to think of myself as honest. Does it bother you?'

'It takes getting used to,' she replied.

They reached a stone parapet overlooking the turquoise sea, and paused to admire the view. The picturesque spot was deserted except for goats grazing on the coarse grass, and taking her hand in his, Jake led Emma down a narrow, stony path to a wooden bench beneath the shade of some trees.

They sat for some moments drinking in the scents of orange blossom and jasmine that floated up from the slopes, but then unfortunately the slight breeze also wafted in their direction the less appealing scent that emanated from the goats.

'Hardly an ideal spot,' Jake remarked, 'but I've been wanting to speak to you alone and this is the first chance I've had. There's no privacy at the villa.'

'You could have come to my room—or are you getting discreet in your old age?'

'You force me to be discreet,' he muttered. 'If I'd come calling on you, you'd have accused me of having dishonourable intentions!'

'That didn't bother you on the last occasion!'

'How little you know.' He frowned and rubbed the side of his face, giving such evident signs of stress that Emma wondered what was wrong with him. 'You're so damn naïve!' he burst out in exasperation. 'You still don't know how I. . . . Look, Emma, the other night, when you were so late and I was worried out of my mind, I realised a few things about myself. Things I didn't want to realise, I'll admit that. But once I did, I couldn't go back to square one.' He turned on the bench and eyed her gravely, moving slowly from her tiny, arched feet to the top of her shiny brown hair. 'You aren't the only one who's changed in the past months, Emma. I have too.'

'Not as much as you'd like me to think, Jake.' Emma's heart was pounding furiously, but she kept her voice cool. 'Or do you expect me to believe that your visits to Celia's bedroom were purely platonic?'

'They were, after the first night.'

'After the. . . . Oh no, I definitely don't believe that!'

'I figured you wouldn't.' His tone was laconic. 'But it happens to be the truth. Celia can't turn me on. No one can except you. Why do you think she's being so nice to Peter? It's only to make me jealous.'

'Oh!' For the life of her, Emma did not know what to say.

'It *is* the truth,' said Jake, his voice more serious than she had ever heard it. 'I knew something odd was happening to me, where you were concerned, but it wasn't until you were out so late the night you went to meet Peter, and I thought you might be dead, that I. . . . God! You've no idea what hell I went through.'

'Not so long ago you were telling me to forget you,' Emma reminded him.

'I know, and I should have heeded my own advice. But unfortunately it's easier to give than to take.' He took her hands in his and held them tightly. 'I've been such a fool, darling. At first I thought it might be amusing to seduce you, but even when I found I couldn't, it took me a while to realise that it was because I loved you.'

'Loved me?' she repeated incredulously. 'You love me?'

'That's what I've been trying to tell you for the past ten minutes,' Jake said wryly. 'The bachelor's been hooked, my darling. The big prowling cat has been caught by a little brown mouse.' He edged closer to her. 'Well, can't you say something.'

'I . . . I don't know what to say.' Although Jake had spoken the words she longed to hear, she had to voice her doubts. 'It wouldn't work,' she whispered. 'We're too different—our values—our way of thinking. . . . I couldn't fit into your kind of life.'

'That's exactly why I want you. *Because* you're different.'

'You'd get bored with me,' she persisted. 'I'm only a novelty to you.'

'No,' he argued. 'It's the other women who bore me. I'm bored with my whole way of life. You've made me see how futile it is.' He pulled her against him. 'Until I met you, I'd never found anyone with whom I wanted to spend the rest of my life. But now I have, and I won't let you get away from me.' His eyes looked deeply into hers, his gaze unswerving. 'I know you love me, Emma. You can't deny it.'

She sighed. 'No, Jake, I can't deny it.'

'Then marry me.'

'Marry you?' she gaped at him in amazement. '*Marry* you?'

'What else did you think I meant?' He saw the answer in her face and looked rueful. 'My darling girl, you're not the mistress type! Whatever gave you that ridiculous idea?'

'You did. I've heard you speak so derisively of marriage. . . .'

'That was before I'd met you.' Jake continued to look at her with gentle wryness. 'Don't tell me you'd agree to live with me without benefit of a ring? If I'd known that, it would have saved me several restless nights while I was making up my mind to ask you to be my wife!'

She laughed. 'I won't let you get out of it now! You've proposed, my darling, and you've burnt your boats.'

'Never to rebuild them,' he added, cupping her chin in the palm of his hand. 'For once in my life I'm thinking not only of what *I* want, but of what *you* want. It's your happiness that concerns me, more than my own, and it's a new experience for me. You must give me time to get used to being unselfish.'

'Oh, Jake,' she said, and put her arms round his neck, burying her face in the collar of his shirt, so that he would not feel the tears of happiness streaking down her cheeks.

He held her tightly and they remained close for a long time, his tender touch telling her more than words how much he loved her.

'So the answer is yes?' he asked finally, his voice low.

'You know you're irresistible—what else could my answer have been?'

His laugh was exuberant and he hugged her with happiness. 'I daren't start kissing you, or I won't want to stop. Oh, Emma, my darling, we're going to be so happy. I hope you don't want a long engagement? I'd like to marry you as soon as it can be arranged. I'll talk to the Consul in Palma and——'

'No, Jake.' Emma pulled away from him. 'Once you go to the Consul it won't be a secret any more.'

'Who wants to keep it a secret?'

'I do—until I've spoken to my grandparents. They'd be awfully hurt if they opened the newspapers and read of it before I had a chance to tell them.'

'Pam will guess the way we feel about each other the minute she sees me looking at you. And so will Peter.'

'Then don't look at me. Please, darling. I'll phone my grandmother tomorrow and break the news. Is that soon enough for you?'

'Yesterday would be even better!'

Emma smiled. 'I still can't help feeling it's all a dream. I thought when you saw me that it was hate at first sight!'

'It was—but then you grew on me.' He stood up. 'I think we'd better make our way back to the car. I'll try not to look too happy—but my acting isn't as good as my writing—and you said my writing's lousy!'

'In that case, you're sure to give the game away!' she mocked, then suddenly chuckled.

'What's the joke?' he asked.

'They say that truth is stranger than fiction. I'm sure no heroine of yours was ever proposed to in a field of goats!'

'I should hope not,' he replied serenely. 'It wouldn't make good Cinerama—only smellerama!' They rounded the corner and heard a short impatient blast from a hooter.

'I think we've been missed,' said Jake, recognising the sound. 'Prepare for some angry words.'

Celia was seething with temper, which exploded the minute Jake and Emma came within earshot.

'Where the hell have you been? We've been sitting baking in this car for hours!'

'Sorry, love,' Jake replied, as he climbed into the driving seat. 'I thought you were exploring the village.'

'That took all of two minutes. I hate these sort of places, anyway—they're all dusty and smelly. Let's drive straight to the hotel.'

'Your wish is my command,' he said, and put the car in gear.

In the back seat, Peter gave Emma a worried look.

'What were you two doing for so long?' he whispered, glancing anxiously at the front to ensure Celia could not hear.

'We were talking to an artist, and forgot the time,' Emma lied.

Fortunately the answer seemed to satisfy him, and within a short while they arrived at the low white building of the Formentor hotel. Set on a bluff of the coastline and surrounded by pinewoods, it was easy to see why the rich and famous found it an ideal retreat. An exquisite garden led down to the sandy beach, where the crystal-clear water lapped gently on to fine gold sand.

But David and Pam were lounging beside one of the swimming pools, glasses of Campari and soda set before them.

'You all look hot and bothered,' Pam remarked with her usual lack of tact. 'We thought you were held up by the traffic.'

'We were held up by Jake and Emma,' Celia said, tightlipped. 'They couldn't drag themselves away from the fascinations of Deya.'

'I'd prefer the fascinations of Celia,' David replied so gallantly that the girl's humour was instantly restored.

Taking advantage of it, Jake suggested she come with him while he ordered lunch, and they went off together. Emma knew he had done it as a deliberate cover-up, but could not help being irritated; which only went to show how illogical she was. She had begged him to keep their plans secret until she had told her own family, and now that he was doing as she asked, she was upset.

'Lobsters and champagne suit everyone?' Jake enquired as he returned to the poolside. 'I think it best if we eat in the dining-room, though. It's air-conditioned.'

'Celebrating something?' Peter asked.

'You don't only drink champagne to celebrate,' Celia said condescendingly.

'I do.'

'That's because you're a fuddy-duddy lawyer, instead of a swinger. You should learn how to enjoy yourself.'

'Why not teach him?' Jake suggested mildly.

Celia looked startled, then gave Emma a triumphant look. 'Do you mind?'

'Of course not.'

The smile on Celia's face made it clear that she thought Emma was lying, and she rose gracefully and caught Peter's arm as they went towards the dining room. 'We'll start our first lesson after lunch, darling. I'm a fantastic teacher!'

By the time the meal was over, three bottles of Moët et Chandon were consumed, and each time Peter's glass emptied, Celia had it refilled. When they rose, his gait was decidedly unsteady.

'Leave him to me,' Celia instructed, giving Emma another triumphant look. 'I'll ask the manager to let him lie down in an empty room.'

'Will you keep him company?' Pam asked with wide-eyed innocence.

'I'll stay with him till he falls asleep.'

Neither Celia nor Peter appeared for the rest of the afternoon, but over pre-dinner cocktails a pale-faced young man rejoined them, apologising to Emma for his disappearance.

'I was quite blotto,' he admitted. 'But fortunately Celia found me a room to lie down in. I hope you weren't upset by my disappearance?'

'Why should I be? I told you, you're a free agent.'

'I know, but I'd hoped——' He broke off and looked at her intently. 'What the hell,' he said waspishly. 'You seem to prefer Jake's company to mine anyway.'

Emma ignored him, and nibbled the olive from her dry Martini. She hoped Peter would not make things difficult when he learned she was going to marry Jake. What a nuisance that he was staying at the villa! Had he been in his own hotel, he would have had an opportunity to meet other girls. She bit her lip, wondering if Jake had influence enough to get him a room in Palma. Her eyes moved to the blond head of the man she loved. Even now she could not believe he wanted to marry her. However often she had thought about it during the course of the afternoon, it still would not sink in. If only she could telephone her grandparents from here and tell them the news. She jumped up swiftly, amazed that she had not thought of it before.

'Been stung?' Pam asked.

'Only by an idea,' Emma laughed. 'I'm going to phone my grandparents now. I haven't spoken to them since I came away.'

'What a clever girl you are,' Jake said promptly, his eyes glittering as blue as the sea. 'You should have thought of it earlier.'

Smiling happily, she hurried away, though her pleasure evaporated when she learned that there was a twenty-four-hour delay on all calls to England, owing to a cable fault at the hotel exchange.

'Don't look so miserable,' Pam consoled her. 'You can phone tomorrow.'

'Pam's right,' said Jake. 'What's a few hours in a lifetime!'

Emma tossed her head. She knew he was teasing her, but somehow resented it. Could he be having second thoughts? She dismissed the idea, but it would not completely vanish, and lay, like undigested food, inside her.

The evening was a triumph for Celia. Dressed to fit her image of a sex goddess, in clinging red satin, slit to the thighs to show her long slender legs, she was the focus of attention—more overtly by the men, whose eyes bulged noticeably as she slunk past them. The hotel was predominantly filled with American and English tourists, most of whom recognised her, and though there was always a fair sprinkling of other celebrities trying their best to look anonymous, Celia was one who certainly did not want to melt into the background!

Several men were bold enough to ask her to dance, and she refused no one. Basking in the heady glow of star status, she seemed unmindful of Jake's lack of attention, though Emma wondered if she were putting on an act, and was genuinely upset by his attitude. Yet how could Celia be genuine about any man?

'It's your turn to dance with me now,' the girl said, swaying in front of David.

'What's wrong with Jake?'

'He bores me.'

David grimaced at his brother. 'You quarrelled with my fair lady?'

'I don't think so,' Jake said easily. 'But Celia loves a row from time to time—even if she has to invent one.'

David rose and escorted Celia to the floor. Peter was already dancing with Pam, and Jake, alone at last with Emma, gave an exaggerated sigh. 'If you wouldn't insist on secrecy, we could be dancing together like a couple of lovebirds!'

'I did try to call home,' she reminded him. 'But if we give ourselves away now, it will be in the British papers by tomorrow.'

'Such is fame,' he sighed, and rose. 'So you stick to your side of the table and I'll stick to mine.'

'Why can't we dance?'

'Because——' Jake stopped. 'Don't ask me to explain or I might shock you.'

'I'm a big girl,' she said softly. 'And not so shockable.'

'Stop it,' he whispered thickly. 'You don't know what you're doing to me.' Their eyes met. 'Well, perhaps you do,' he smiled, and deliberately turned away from her and gave his attention to the people on the dance floor.

By the time they returned to the villa it was nearly one,

and surprisingly a light was still on in the lounge. As they opened the front door, Nanny hurried into the hall to meet them.

'Is something wrong with Toby?' Pam asked instantly.

'No, Mrs Sanders, he's fine.' She turned to Emma. 'I'm afraid it's your grandfather. Your grandmother telephoned this afternoon and said he'd had a heart attack and is in the intensive care unit of the local hospital.'

Emma clutched at the hall table for support. Immediately Peter went to her side, but she looked past him to Jake.

'I must go home immediately.'

'Of course. But first we'll try to call them. It shouldn't be difficult at this time of the morning.'

Within minutes Emma was talking to her grief-stricken grandmother, who was almost incoherent with strain.

'Come home as soon as you can,' she sobbed. 'I hope he lasts until you get here.'

'I'll catch the first flight I can,' Emma promised. 'Don't cry, darling. I'm sure everything will be fine—I feel it in my bones.'

'I'll try to get you a seat first thing in the morning,' Jake told her as she rang off. 'I've some influence at the airport—and if *I* can't get you on a plane, no one will.'

'I'd like to return with her,' said Peter. 'Could you try to get me a seat as well?'

'There's no need for you to come with me,' Emma protested, and threw Jake a pleading glance, hoping he himself would suggest coming with her. But he didn't, and Peter reiterated his own intention of leaving, insisting that he wanted to be with her in case the worst happened.

'You're so kind,' she said huskily.

'I feel almost part of your family,' he reminded her. 'I've known your grandparents all my life.'

Emma glanced past Peter to where Jake was standing

by the window. He seemed aloof from the situation, and fear clutched at her. But she could not think of herself and Jake now, when her grandfather was so ill, and she went upstairs to pack her things.

She had finished one case, and had stopped to cool off because it was so hot, when there was a gentle knock at the door and Jake came in.

'My poor darling,' he said at once, gathering her into his arms. 'What an ending to a perfect day!'

She sighed and relaxed against him. 'I wish *you'd* suggested flying back with me,' she murmured. 'Why did you leave it to Peter?'

'Because he knows your grandparents—as he said. I'd be a stranger to them, Emma. Worse, even—a celebrity stranger. Your grandmother wouldn't want me around at a time like this. She'd start thinking of you marrying me and moving away from England, and she'd feel even worse than she does now.'

It was such a logical explanation for his not coming with her that Emma was staggered she had not thought of it herself.

'Did you think I'd got cold feet about us?' he questioned, and seeing the answer in her eyes, looked angry.

'I'm sorry, Jake, I've been very stupid.'

'You certainly have. I want to shout my love for you from the rooftops, not deny it. Don't you know that?'

He went to kiss her, but she drew back. What he had said a moment ago had alerted her to the problems that their marriage would bring to her grandparents—more particularly to her grandmother, should her grandfather die. It was something she had to tell Jake at once.

'What you said about being a celebrity and not living in England. . . . It means I wouldn't be near them, doesn't it?'

'Not unless they lived abroad too,' he said gently. 'What

are you trying to say, Emma? That you don't want to tell them about us for the moment?' He read the answer on her face, and caught her close again. 'I've waited thirty-three years for the right girl, my darling, so I suppose I can be patient for a while longer.'

'Oh, Jake!' she cried. 'You're beginning to know me so well that I'll never be able to have any secrets from you.'

Laughing softly, he began to kiss her, his lips pressing firmly on hers and forcing them apart. Then, as if she were a feather. he lifted her in his arms and placed her gently on the bed.

She smiled up lovingly and twined her arms around his neck as he lowered himself carefully beside her. He nibbled at her ear, then kissed the nape of her neck, swiftly undoing the tiny buttons of her dress to run his lips down her throat into the hollow of her breasts. Emma could feel his heart pounding as his breath quickened with excitement, and his hands reached beneath her to undo the clasp of her bra. Released, her breasts lay creamy white, like two pears against the deep tan of her body.

'You're even more lovely than I remembered,' Jake whispered as he drank in her beauty.

Light as a butterfly, his lips caressed each rosy tip, arousing her to a fever pitch of passion, and her hands went beneath his silk shirt to rake his back with her fingers.

'Jake, Jake,' she murmured, 'I've never felt this way before.'

He moved slightly and cupped her face in the palms of his hands, kissing each corner of her mouth tenderly, until he covered it once again with his own, arousing her further, until she was hypnotically abandoned and ready to submit to anything to assuage her longing and his.

With a groan Jake pushed himself away from her, and got off the bed, running a shaky hand through his hair.

'Cover yourself, darling,' he said huskily, 'or I shan't be responsible for my actions.'

Emma reddened as she realised she was half naked, and she hurriedly drew the sheet around her and gave Jake a shy smile. 'I know it's silly of me, but I didn't feel at all embarrassed while you were making love to me, yet now I do.'

'That's because you're an adorable little innocent,' he replied tenderly, and bent down to kiss the top of her head. 'Regrettably, it looks as if you're going to stay that way for the time being—I have my conscience to thank for that!'

Emma slid off the bed, trailing the sheet behind her as she clutched the ends to stop them falling. 'It will be all the better for waiting,' she replied.

'I can tell you with absolute certainly,' he said gravely, 'that there's no truth at all in *that* theory!'

He caught her to him again and pressed his lips to the nape of her neck in a gesture that was full of love—not passion. As always his touch sent a shiver of excitement down her spine, making it impossible for her to think of anything but his closeness. She knew Jake was aware of her response—but he did not take advantage of it.

'*This* is to remember me by,' he whispered, his mouth against her lips. 'Come back to me very soon, sweetheart.'

When he had gone, Emma found it impossible to sleep. Although distressed by her grandfather's heart attack, she could not help experiencing a deep sense of warmth at the prospect of her life with Jake. And her grandparents would love him too. She was sure of it. How her grandmother would show off to all her friends that her granddaughter had captured such a famous celebrity! Please let Grandfather live to enjoy my happiness, she prayed, and bent her head in supplication.

Even after she had prayed, she was still too excited and

restless to sleep. Anxiety mingled with the emotions Jake had aroused, and she pushed back the cover and got out of bed. Not bothering to put her contact lenses in, she fumbled her way into the garden. If only she could tell someone about her love for Jake! She flung her arms wide. The air was still, not a tree or a bush moved. Even the cicadas slept in the heat of the balmy Mediterranean night. Stars winked conspiratorially at her from the midnight blue heavens, as if they knew her secret too.

Seating herself on one of the hammocks, she swung back and forth to create a slight breeze. Suddenly she froze and placed her feet firmly on the ground to stop the movement. Celia's voice floated down from the terrace of her room above.

'Darling, you were wonderful—the best ever.'

Emma could not hear the man's reply, only the murmur of a deeper voice and then Celia's laugh, before she spoke again.

'You're insatiable, darling! But that's your attraction, isn't it? A man whose appetites match my own.'

Emma's heart skipped a beat, and a feeling of such pain passed through her that she started to shake.

So Jake had not been able to control his passion after all. He had gone straight from her arms to Celia's. She buried her face in her trembling hands, and tears of sadness and anger flowed down her cheeks.

Standing up, she peered at the balcony, but could only make out two blurred shapes, however hard she blinked her eyes. Damn! Why hadn't she put in her lenses? But then perhaps it was better this way. Why torture herself with the sight of Celia in Jake's arms? Imagining it was bad enough.

She stepped back into the shadows. In her heart of hearts wasn't this what she had been frightened of? How could she have hoped to keep a man like Jake happy and monogamous? But she had not expected him to be faithless quite so soon, and had believed him when he had told her that his affair with Celia was over. What an innocent she still was! Jake might not love Celia, but like an addict his body still craved her, and he was not prepared to cut her out of his life completely. Perhaps he could not, for all his pretence to the contrary.

She did not doubt that he loved her in his way—and was sincere in his wish to marry her. Why else had he asked her when he could have chosen almost any woman he wanted? Evidently her naïvety and old-fashioned morality had appealed to him—and she knew why. He had to settle down one day—it was a natural thing for a man to desire a stable home life with a wife and children—and she had evidently come along at just the right time. She was also eminently suitable. Not too pretty, an excellent housekeeper and cook and, best of all in his eyes, refreshingly innocent. She managed a rueful smile. Not a bad reference if she wanted to apply for a similar position!

But she would not accept a compromise marriage, however much she longed to be his wife. It must be all or nothing.

Her tears flowed faster, and wearily she returned to her room, flinging herself face down on the pillows and allowing the sobs to rack her body. Her dreams had been shattered in a day—and turned into a nightmare.

In the morning she would have to tell Jake she knew. Her mind was resolute that she could not and would not marry him now—but she was frightened that his power over her was so great that he would persuade her that his bedding of Celia had been only a momentary lapse—perhaps brought on by frustration caused by his wish not to make love to Emma until they were married. She knew him well enough to know he would use any ploy to get what he wanted and, since words were his forte, he would make good use of them to gain the upper hand.

But he won't make me change my mind, Emma vowed. I'll love him all my life, but I'll never marry him. Yet no matter who else I meet or marry, he will always be the man on the horizon—the Prince Charming who nearly made me his princess; who showed me his glimpse of heaven and then closed the door.

CHAPTER ELEVEN

AFTER a sleepless night Emma was the first one down in the morning, and heavy-hearted, prepared her last breakfast. It might as well have been the Last Supper, with Jake as her Judas—though there would be no resurrecting their love affair.

Carmen clucked sympathetically at her when she came through the back door. 'Nanny she tell me you go home today. I miss you, Emma. You very good cook and nice girl.'

Emma smiled her thanks and busied herself trimming the bacon. By the time the coffee had percolated Jake came in to tell her he had managed to get a booking on the noon flight.

'They had one first class and one tourist,' he said, 'and naturally I took the first class seat for you. They're charging it to me.'

'No, please, I'd rather pay for it myself.'

'Don't be silly, darling.'

'I'm not silly!'

'Yes, you are. I'm *entitled* to pay your fare home,' he said with a smile. 'That was part of my agreement when I employed you.'

'It wasn't part of the agreement to fly me first class.'

His smile disappeared. 'What's the matter with you, Emma?' He came up and stood behind her, his head resting on hers, oblivious of Carmen's curious stare.

'Nothing,' Emma replied, whisking the eggs in the stainless steel bowl.

'Don't lie.' He turned her round to face him, and noticed the tears brimming at the edge of her eyes. Mistaking the reason for them, he said tenderly: 'I'm sure you'll find things aren't so bad once you get back. Don't think the worst, darling. Your grandfather's in intensive care, so he's getting the best possible treatment.'

Emma shrugged his hand from her arm and turned back to the counter top. His nearness made her long to shelter in the strength of his arms in spite of his treachery, and only level-headed common sense—something she might often despise but in this instance was grateful for—stopped her from doing so.

'Please leave me alone, Jake,' she murmured. 'I want to give Carmen some instructions.'

'Don't worry about that,' he said swiftly. 'I'll telephone an agency I know in London and they'll fly a cook out to me. I've used them before in an emergency.'

Emma's tears flowed faster. How quickly her place here would be filled—a cook in the kitchen and Celia in his bed. What an organiser Jake was!

'Come and have some breakfast,' he pleaded. 'Carmen's quite capable of making toast and coffee.'

'I'm not hungry,' Emma said, 'and I've some last-minute packing to do.'

Accepting her urge to be left alone, Jake went out, and Emma retired to her room and stayed there until it was nearly time to leave the villa, then she went down to the patio, where Jake and his brother were sitting, while Pam played with Toby on the edge of the lawn.

'You look tired,' Pam remarked sympathetically.

'I didn't get much sleep last night,' Emma admitted. 'I felt so restless that I went out in the garden.' She threw a look in Jake's direction, but his eyes remained relaxed.

'That's funny,' Pam said. 'David couldn't sleep either and went out for a walk. He was gone ages.' She gave him an affectionate glance. 'I bet you had a secret rendezvous with Emma!'

'How clever of you to guess,' he replied. 'She's been teaching me to cook!'

'So you can lend Carmen a hand, then,' Pam said promptly, and came over to Emma. 'I know I promised Jake I wouldn't say anything—but I can't help myself. He told us you're coming back to marry him and we're delighted. We hoped he'd come to his senses one day and settle down, but we never imagined he'd have the good sense to choose a girl like you.'

'I'm sorry to disappoint you,' Emma replied, 'but I'm not marrying Jake.'

'You're not . . .?' Pam looked at Jake, who had risen and was advancing on Emma.

'What are you talking about?' he asked, his voice low.

'I'm not going to marry you,' Emma reiterated as firmly as her trembling lips would allow.

'Since when? Yesterday you——'

'Let's talk about last night instead,' she cut in. 'You went straight from my room to Celia's. Don't bother to deny it—I was sitting in the garden and I overheard you.'

'You *what?*'

'Don't pretend!' Emma said. 'It's all over . . . finished. I hate the sight of you!'

'For God's sake, stop talking like a fool!'

He reached out for her, but she stepped back, shaking like a leaf.

'No, Jake, I won't change my mind. It's all over.'

'Not until you've heard me out.' He threw a quick look at his brother, and then pleaded with Emma again, 'Let's talk about this on our own.'

'*No!*' She backed further away. 'It's too late. I'm going to marry Peter as soon as it can be arranged,' she lied recklessly, praying Peter would not appear and overhear her.

'You're crazy!' Jake shouted. 'And a liar into the bargain.'

'I'm not lying. My grandparents like him, and I'm going to listen to them. I should have done so long ago, instead of coming here and letting you make love to me.'

Pam and David made a move to leave, but Jake swung round and stopped them. 'You've no need to go. If Emma wants to think badly of me, let her.'

'I don't *want* to,' she cried, 'but I have no choice.'

'If you had love,' he retorted, 'you wouldn't need choice. But you're prepared to condemn me without a hearing, and if that's your idea of trust. . . .'

'Don't talk to me of trust! In my book that means faithfulness, and you couldn't even stay faithful on the day you proposed! Nothing you can say will ever make me forget that!' Turning on her heel, she sped towards the house.

'Go after her, Jake,' Pam pleaded.

'Never!' Emma heard him say. 'We're through.'

As Emma reached the inner hall, Peter came down the stairs, case in hand.

'We'd better be leaving,' he said. 'You all right?'

She nodded, not trusting herself to speak, and he went out to the patio, returning almost at once with David, who had the car keys in his hand.

'Sure you won't see Jake alone for a minute?' David asked her.

'Positive.' She went out to the car and climbed in, resolutely averting her head from the villa as they drove down the curving driveway. How easily Jake had let her go! Had he really cared for her, he would have insisted on seeing her alone; forced her, if words had failed. But he had accepted her rejection with only a token share of anger; almost as if he were glad she was turning him down.

It was not until she and Peter were in the Customs hall waiting to board the plane that he tentatively asked her what was upsetting her.

'It's more than just your grandfather's attack,' he added. 'When I went out to the patio to say goodbye, Pam was in tears, and Jake looked like thunder. What is it, Emma? Don't play me for an idiot. I'm entitled to know the truth.'

'You are,' she said contritely, 'and I'd have told you anyway, even if you hadn't asked me.' She drew a deep breath. 'Jake asked me to marry him, but I turned him down.'

'I see. So that's why he looked so furious. I'm glad you had the sense, Emma. At one point I thought he'd bowled you over.'

She could not bring herself to say she was still bowled over, and she blinked the tears from her eyes. Was it wounded pride that prevented her telling Peter the whole truth? She did not analyse her feelings. She only knew it was impossible to repeat what she had overheard and dimly seen last night in the garden.

'You'd never have made a go of it with him,' Peter went on, covering one of her small hands with his own. 'He's a good-looking chap, and with his money and glamour it was only natural you'd fall for him. But his life-style isn't yours, and you've had a lucky get-out—even though you don't think it right now. But in a few weeks you'll see things more realistically—and then I'll be waiting.'

'Not for *me*,' she said at once, coming out of her reverie. 'I couldn't possibly marry you, Peter. Not now. I don't love you.'

'You may change your mind,' he said stubbornly.

Emma decided not to argue. It was best to let time show him she meant what she said. However, she was relieved when they were separated on the journey, she in first class, and Peter behind in tourist. At least it gave her time to collect her thoughts.

She had hoped that Jake would come to the airport and beg her forgiveness. But of course he hadn't. Take me as I am or not at all—that was his way. Perhaps she should have spoken to him on his own, at least heard his version—or rather his excuse. But what would have been the point? It was better to cut him out of her life completely.

At least she was a more independent person than the one who had left England two months ago. Jake had made her grow up quickly—and for that she would always be grateful.

The next few weeks passed swiftly, with Emma and her grandmother visiting the hospital every day. She determinedly refused to think about the future—or what she would do when her grandfather was home again. She only knew she could not stay in Oakton.

To her surprise Jake telephoned twice, but each time she refused to speak to him, telling Rachel, the housekeeper, to say she was out. Her grandmother made no attempt to hide her curiosity, but did not question her, knowing Emma would tell her everything when the time was right, as in fact it was on the day her grandfather came out of hospital. Even so, she glossed over the depth of her hurt, and pretended she had broken her engagement to Jake because she was uncertain of being happy to lead the sort of life he did.

'He's a very handsome young man,' her grandmother commented. 'I saw his picture on the jacket of his last book. Are you sure you aren't making a mistake, my dear? If you love each other, he may well decide not to travel around so much.'

'His life would still be too glamorous for me,' Emma stated. 'And I'd hate having to compete for his attention with a hundred other girls.'

'Why should he want to marry *you* if he still wanted other girls?' came the innocent question, and Emma gave a broken laugh.

'Because men like Jake always enjoy conquering new fields,' she said. 'He isn't the faithful type like Grandfather. It's not the fashion these days.'

'Then you're well rid of him.'

'That's what I keep telling myself. But I can't make myself believe it.' Emma paused. 'I'll probably find it easier when I'm occupied with a job, and that means going to London, I'm afraid. I'll never find anything worthwhile down here.'

'In cookery, you mean?' her grandmother asked.

'That's what I'm trained for. I daresay I'll join a catering firm or become a demonstrator.'

'Why not open your own restaurant? I'm sure you'd enjoy it much more than working for somebody else.'

'I'm sure I would too,' Emma said dryly, 'but there are two things against it. One, I'd need someone to come in with me and share the workload—someone I can trust. And two, I'd need a hell of a lot of money to get it going.'

'What about your friend Sally Wilson? Didn't she want you to open a restaurant with her at one time?'

'Yes, but it was just a pipe dream and we both knew it.'

'Would she still be interested in joining you?'

'Going into partnership with me, you mean?' Emma asked.

Her grandmother nodded. 'I've noticed a big difference in you since you've been home, and your grandfather and I have been talking things over.' The old lady settled back against the wing chair in which she was sitting. 'First, we've decided to go and live in an old people's home. Rachel wants to retire—and frankly I can't take the responsibility of looking after Grandpa—I'm too old for that.' She held up her hand as Emma started to protest. 'We've spoken to Dr Summers and he thinks it's an excellent idea, and knows the ideal place for us. We'll sell the house, and with the money we already have, it will be more than enough to see us out for the rest of our days, and still leave a sizeable amount for you.'

'I don't want anything,' Emma cried. 'Spend it all on yourselves, for heaven's sake.'

'We're too old to do that,' her grandmother smiled. 'Besides, we'll enjoy it much more if we can give it to you while we're alive. And we'd like to start by letting you have enough to open your own restaurant—if that's what you want.'

'What I *want*?' Emma gasped. 'Why, it's what I've dreamed of!'

And so it was. Short of being Jake's wife, running her own restaurant was the one thing guaranteed to give her zest for living. For the first time in weeks, her depression lifted and, too moved to speak, she put her arms around her grandmother's frail shoulders.

Before the day was out, Emma had contacted Sally, who was as keen as ever to join forces with her, and also spoke to an estate agent in the nearby town.

She had always felt the district could sustain a good

restaurant, because apart from being a tourist attraction, it was near enough to London for people to drive out to eat. Added to which, her grandparents were moving to an old people's home in the vicinity, and it would be an advantage to be near them.

Within a week she had found what she was looking for, and within a month contracts had been exchanged on a shop in the High Street. It had an eighteenth-century bow-front, which they retained, as they did the oak-beamed interior and polished floors. But the kitchen which they built in was strictly twentieth century, as were the rest of the fixtures and fittings. Converting was an expensive job, but Emma was supremely confident that the restaurant would be a success, and had no qualms at spending the money.

In this she was proved right.

Sally, her partner, was capable and knowledgeable, and had many trade connections. She had been a teacher at the Cordon Bleu School during the time Emma had gone there, and was the one who ensured they had a write-up in the London evening papers soon after opening. It was so flattering about their menus and service that *Harper's* and *The Times* swiftly followed suit, which brought increased business beyond their wildest dreams.

Dame Fortune continued to smile on them; for their first summer the weather was exceptionally warm, and the fourteen tables were continually booked for lunch and dinner. It was exceedingly hard work, but Emma loved it. She lost herself completely when she cooked, and gave full vent to her creativity by inventing exciting and original dishes.

But however busy she was, no day passed without thought of Jake. She had hoped that time would help her to forget him, but the ache continued. She avidly read the papers for any mention of his name, and was all too easily able to follow the life he was leading.

He was a natural target for publicity. Not a week passed without her seeing his picture smiling at her, with a new girl beside him. None of them seemed to last for long, and none of them seemed to make him happy, for he was always flitting from place to place—Majorca, New York, Los Angeles and London.

The only good news in Emma's life—apart from the success of the restaurant—was that Peter finally accepted that she would not marry him, and after a brief courtship with the local show-jumping champion, announced his engagement.

Emma was invited to the party, and although it was difficult for her to get away—the restaurant was open seven days a week in the summer—she felt it would be churlish to refuse. After the last meal had been served, she quickly changed and drove to the home of the bride-to-be.

'I hear you're getting a write-up in one of the Sunday supplements,' Peter said, after the obligatory kiss and murmurs of congratulations.

'Good news travels fast!' Emma replied with a smile, and sipped her champagne.

'How did it come about?'

'Pure luck. The editor himself came down for a meal, and enjoyed it so much that he suggested it to us.'

'You've really made a go of it,' Peter said admiringly. 'Though from the look of you, you're working too hard.'

'Thanks,' said Emma. 'Does that mean I look a wreck?'

He shook his head. 'Never that. But you're too thin and your eyes are big as saucers.' He hesitated, then said in a quiet voice, 'Ever hear from Jake?'

'Not a word.' She marvelled that she could sound so casual. 'We didn't exactly part on the friendliest of terms, did we? And from what I read in the papers, he hasn't been pining for me.'

'His new film seems to be doing well in the States.'

'You know the old saying—the rich get richer. . . .'

Peter gave her a penetrating look. 'You're not still in love with him, are you?'

'Don't be silly! I haven't given him a thought for months. The restaurant takes up all my time, and that's the way I prefer it.'

She almost made herself believe it when she saw the wonderful centre spread on their restaurant, in the Sunday magazine three weeks later. Proudly she took a copy with her when she went to visit her grandparents, and they showed it off with pride to all and sundry at the home, and basked in the reflected glory.

'You look far too young and pretty to be so capable,' her grandfather praised her, as he peered at her photo for the umpteenth time.

'I don't always cook in a hundred-pound dress,' Emma grinned. 'I only put it on while my picture was being taken.'

'You'd look beautiful whatever you wore!'

But beauty did not matter in the weeks following the article—only hard work did, and Emma and Sally had to extend their hours to accommodate all the bookings.

'We might as well make hay while the sun shines,' Sally said after one particularly hectic evening. 'In this business you never know how long success can last—however good your food is. Next year the weather might be disastrous and no one will drive out here for a meal.'

'We're sufficiently well known not to rely on the London trade now,' Emma pointed out.

'Mmm. . . .' Sally was absorbed in a letter she was reading, and not paying attention. 'What shall we do about this?' she asked, waving the letter at Emma.

Emma stopped stirring the hollandaise sauce and took

it off the gas before reaching out for the sheet of thick cream paper. Quickly she read it.

'I don't see why we can't agree,' she murmured, rubbing her neck tiredly. 'If he wants to book the entire restaurant for his engagement, let him. Obviously money is no object, from what he says, and with a set menu for forty people we can make far more than if we opened as usual for the evening.'

'In that case I'll send Mr Andaker the estimate he asks for by return. Let's sit down and work out what food to give him. As you said money is no object, so we can really go to town.'

When Sally left the kitchen to type out their reply, Emma read Jess Andaker's letter again. It was undoubtedly most flattering.

'Having read and heard so many excellent reports of your restaurant, I feel it would be the ideal setting for my engagement. I shall leave the menu and wines to you, and merely wish you to know that money is no object, and that I want the best that your expertise can provide. All I shall arrange is for flowers to be sent from Moyses Stevens in London, and you can expect my arrival at eight, on the date mentioned. Please let me know costs, and I will send a cheque by return of post.'

True to his word, he did, making no comment on the food they had chosen, other than to say he had given them an additional hundred pounds to cover unexpected expenses.

'I think we'll make sure the bank clears his cheque before we order the food and champagne,' Sally said practically. 'You never know—it could be a hoax.'

But it wasn't. The cheque was cleared and, all fears allayed, they happily set about the preparations for the party. They had drawn up an interesting menu: cornets of smoked salmon filled with scampi for the hors d'oeuvres, followed by cream of courgette soup. Next came quail roasted on the spit and served with wild rice, raisins and almonds, and a choice of three desserts: prâline soufflé, fresh fig tart and English strawberries with crème fraiche.

'I wonder what Mr Andaker's fiancée is like?' Sally asked, putting the finishing touches to the prâline soufflé before setting it in the refrigerator. 'I bet she doesn't even know she's having a party for her engagement.'

'I'd hate that,' Emma replied. 'Surprises are fine, but looking forward to a party, and planning it, is all part of the fun.'

'And the headaches too. Personally I'd rather fancy being married to a man who takes charge of everything.' Dreamily Sally looked into the distance, coming back to the present only as the outer door bell rang. 'That must be the flowers arriving,' she said. 'I wonder what he chose?'

Moments later she rushed back, her face agleam. 'Do come and see them, Emma,' she urged. 'They're fabulous!'

Wiping her hands on a towel, Emma straightened and yawned. She was not tired, yet she felt curiously listless. Preparing for someone else's engagement had reminded her forcibly of her own brief day of happiness, when the future had looked so rosy. Now it stretched bleakly ahead of her—long days of hard work. True, she enjoyed it, but it was work nonetheless—with no prospect of anything other than a marriage to which she could only give part of her heart; Jake still had the rest of it. Faithless, uncaring Jake.

'Come *on*,' Sally repeated, 'do come and look.'

Slowly Emma went into the restaurant. The sight that met her eyes was so dazzling that all other thoughts were instantly wiped from her mind.

On every one of the fourteen tables, a shallow gold

wicker basket spilled a mass of orchids, roses and carnations in a profusion of colours, while eight tall white urns, each filled with some exotic kind of flowering tree, had been set around the walls. Standing beside the door was a young man in jeans, holding a tiny basket of miniature red roses, each petal as smooth as silk. Nestling in the centre was a black velvet box.

'The ring!' Sally breathed. 'Oooh, I bet that's a surprise for the girl too. Isn't it romantic, Emma?'

'It might not fit her,' Emma said practically.

'That's a minor detail. What a misery you are!'

Emma forced a smile, knowing Sally was right. Just because she was miserable there was no reason to spoil her friend's enjoyment of the occasion. After all, they had both worked like Trojans to make a superlative dinner, and they might as well savour some of the pleasure—if not the food.

'What's the ring like?' she asked the young man.

Carefully he opened the box to reveal an enormous pear-shaped diamond.

'*That* didn't come from Moyses Stevens,' Sally quipped.

'From Cartier's, actually,' came the reply. 'I had to deliver it personally for insurance coverage.'

Sally peered closely at it, then lifted it out of the box and gave a low, unladylike whistle as it sparkled blue white on her finger.

'It must have cost a fortune,' she remarked.

'Twenty thousand pounds,' he confided. 'I assume there'll be someone here all day, otherwise I have to stay with it.'

'There's no need,' Emma reassured him. 'We'll guard it with our lives!'

'Twenty thousand pounds on a ring,' Sally murmured when they were alone. 'Mr Andaker must be a millionaire.'

'And a fool,' Emma replied. 'Who else would spend that much on a lump of carbon!'

'You wouldn't say that if it was your lump of carbon!'

'Perhaps not,' Emma agreed, half smiling, knowing that Jake would never have thought of such a romantic idea as this party. Those sort of things only happened in his books. In his real life he was practical and forthright—and faithless.

'I wonder if she's as rich as he is?' Sally mused.

'Who?' Emma enquired, her thoughts miles away with Jake, whose last newspaper picture had flashed across the wires from Los Angeles, where he was signing a contract to write a script for a multi-million-dollar epic that was going to topple James Bond from the screen.

'The lucky girl,' Sally said. 'That's who. I bet she's some hardboiled little bit with a face like a pumpkin. That sort often snag the richest men.'

'More likely she's a young girl selling herself to a man old enough to be her father,' Emma replied. 'Which is probably why Mr Andaker's gone overboard for her!'

'Overboard and diving for sunken treasure,' Sally giggled. 'He'll need it if he intends to continue treating Mrs Andaker like this!'

Emma laughed and, still amused by the thought, they both returned to the kitchen to carry on cooking. It was a long, tiring day, even though much of the preparation had been done ahead of time. But as the evening approached, their work slackened, and Emma began to feel an unexpected sense of pleasure in the happenings ahead. At least let her enjoy someone else's happiness; it was better than having none at all.

Fifteen minutes before Mr Andaker and his party were due, she went into the dining room for a final inspection. Sally had stage-managed the scene perfectly. The pink-clothed tables with their matching napkins and gleaming glass and silverware were enhanced by the flowered centrepieces, around which stood slender red candles in glass holders.

The light from them reflected on the dark beams of the ceiling and flickered and danced as if the celebrations had already begun.

'The perfume is heavenly,' Emma said softly, looking at the mass of flowers banked around the room. 'They certainly improve the place. Perhaps we should put in a permanent order!'

'Only if we want to make a permanent loss!' Sally chuckled. 'This little lot would set us back a month's profit.'

'I know, and the sad thing is they'll all be dead in the morning. Once the room fills up, the heat will kill them.' Emma stopped speaking as she heard the screech of brakes on the road outside. 'They're arriving. Quick, take off your apron!'

'What for? Let Mr Andaker see how hard we've been working. He may even give us a bonus!'

Sally stood her ground and Emma, hiding her amusement at her friend's practical suggestion, remained beside her. A car door slammed, footsteps crossed the cobbled pavement and the door opened.

Framed by the dark beams stood the most handsome man Emma had seen. Tall, broad-shouldered, with bronzed skin and thick hair the colour of a gold coin. Even in the romantic glow of candlelight, the colour of his eyes—blue as summer skies—was devastatingly apparent, as was the flash of white teeth as he smiled and strode over, elegant in white dinner jacket and black trousers.

'Hullo, Emma,' said Jake.

She opened her mouth to speak, but no words came out. She swallowed, but still had difficulty moving her tongue.

'I can see I've surprised you,' he said smoothly. 'But I've booked here for dinner.'

She swallowed again. 'You're out of luck, I'm afraid. Every table's engaged.'

'So am I,' he answered. 'It's *my* party.'

Wildly she stared at him. '*Yours?* But—your name . . . the cheque. . . .'

'I see you still don't do anagrams—it's another one for Jake Sanders. I knew you'd never accept my booking if I did it under my own name. And as for the cheque—that was easily arranged with my bank. I thought it was an amusing idea.'

'Why, you—you. . . .' Words failed her.

What a heartless trick to play! She had never imagined revenge to be part of his nature, but nothing else could explain his action. She was in no doubt that he knew she was part-owner of the restaurant, even though his letter had been addressed to Sally. That was why he had shown no surprise at seeing her. In fact, he appeared as unruffled as if they had parted yesterday on the best of terms.

With an effort she controlled her temper. 'You're full of amusing ideas, aren't you? And holding your engagement here is particularly hilarious. Who's the lucky girl?'

'An idiot.'

'I beg your pardon!'

'So you should,' he said forcefully. 'If you'd had a modicum of common sense, this last lousy year could have been completely avoided.'

'Would someone mind telling me what's going on?' Sally pleaded, and Jake gave her one of his bewitching smiles.

'I'm trying to tell my fiancée that she needlessly put us both on the rack—and I don't mean rack of lamb!'

'Oh, stop it!' Emma cried, near to tears. 'If this is your idea of a joke, I want no part of it.'

'It's no joke, Emma.' Jake advanced on her, looking taller

than ever above her. 'I love you, and I'm going to marry you.'

'Never!'

'For *ever*,' he corrected. 'Yes, my darling. For the rest of my life. Only you.' He cast a pleading look at Sally, who took the hint and disappeared into the kitchen. 'Now then,' he said softly, 'where was I?'

'On your way out. If you think you're going to talk me round, you're out of your mind!'

'I certainly am out of it,' he agreed. 'I've been that way practically from the minute I met you. Oh, Emma, why didn't you give me a chance to explain?'

'Because I don't like your stories,' she cried furiously, 'and I didn't want to listen to another one of them. Now get out! Get out before I call Peter!' she added wildly.

'Peter who?' he asked, smiling.

'My husband,' she flared. 'We're married and——'

'Little liar,' Jake interrupted, coming so close that he was almost touching her breasts. His eyes burned into her with an intensity of desire that set her pulses racing, and the familiar weakness of loving him and wanting him permeated her bones. 'Little liar,' he repeated. 'Pam sent me the announcement of his engagement together with the article about you in that Sunday magazine. That's why I'm here.'

As he spoke, she studied him closely, aware that beneath his tan he looked older and less carefree. Lines etched his once smooth forehead, and smaller ones fanned out beneath his eyes.

'Nothing has changed between us,' she replied harshly. 'You had no right to come here.'

'Yes, I have. I've booked your services for the evening, and that's what I'm going to have.' He reached out and pushed her into a chair. 'Now sit still and listen to me.'

He looked menacing enough to force her, and she sat quiet.

'Very well,' she muttered. 'Say what you want and then go.'

'When you've heard me out—which you refused to do before—you may ask me to stay.' He gave a brief smile. 'We'll talk about your last night at the villa.'

'No!'

'Yes,' he said firmly. 'You accused me of going from your room to Celia's, and when I denied it, you chose not to believe me.'

'You didn't make your denial very convincing.'

'I was afraid to. At least not while Pam was there.' He paused. 'You see, I thought it was David with Celia.'

Emma raised her head and stared at him. '*David?* I don't believe it!'

'Well, when Pam mentioned that he'd left his room to go for a stroll—and you hadn't met him, although you were also in the garden—I put two and two together and made five. I knew it hadn't occurred to Pam, though—she naturally assumed it was me with Celia—and I couldn't say anything to arouse her suspicions. One wrong word from me would have ruined a perfectly happy marriage. But of course you wouldn't give me the chance to speak to you alone.'

'Why didn't you come after me?' Emma demanded. 'You let me leave the villa thinking you were——'

'I didn't care what the hell you thought!' he interrupted violently. 'I was so angry at your lack of faith, I could have throttled you. If you couldn't trust me before we were married, what chance did I have afterwards? I hoped I could live without you, and I've tried damned hard. But I can't, Emma. I love you too much.'

Emma felt as if the world were topsy-turvy. So it hadn't been Jake with Celia! All the misery she had suffered this last year had been for nothing.

'So it was David,' she murmured.

'No, it wasn't,' Jake said abruptly.

Emma looked at him, unable to take in what he was saying. Somehow it wasn't important. All that mattered was that it had not been Jake.

'It wasn't David either,' he repeated. 'When I spoke to him after he returned from taking you to the airport, he flatly denied it. In fact he laughed at me. That only left one other person.'

'Peter!' Emma exclaimed, and the pieces suddenly fell into place. 'It must have started that afternoon in Formentor. Oh, why didn't he admit it?'

'Did he know you suspected *me*?'

'No. I only told him I'd quarrelled with you, but I didn't give him any reason. If only I had?' she cried, and began to tremble violently.

'Still want to throw me out?' Jake asked, drawing her to her feet. 'Don't be too angry with yourself, darling. I had a pretty wild reputation, and you were so scared of me half the time that you didn't know how to judge me.'

'Your behaviour with Celia didn't help,' she snapped.

'That was all talk and no action,' he reminded her. 'That's why she was so bitchy with me, and turned her attentions to Peter.'

'Poor Peter,' Emma murmured. 'I didn't want him, so he made do with Celia.'

'She'd love you for saying that,' Jake said dryly. 'But let's not waste time talking about either of them. It's us I'm concerned with.'

'What about us?'

Jake pressed his face against hers. 'Marry me soon, Emma. I can't go on like this. I've worked and played like the devil to try to get you out of my system, but nothing could satisfy my need for you.'

'I just worked,' she said dryly, and pulled back from his hold.

'What's the matter?' he asked. 'Don't prevaricate, Emma. From now on there has to be total honesty between us.'

'Very well.' She drew a breath. 'I love you, Jake. More now than before, if that's possible. But I'm scared of it. It makes me jealous and vulnerable.'

'Vulnerable?'

'Afraid,' she explained. 'You meet so many beautiful women in your profession that I'll never be able to relax.'

'What a child you are,' he said tenderly, tracing the curve of her cheek with his fingers. 'If I were only interested in a pretty face, I could have had my pick of dozens. But I want more than that. That's why I'm begging you to marry me—yes, my darling, *begging*. Once I fell for you, I was spoiled for anyone else.' He wrapped his arms around her, holding her body tightly to his own. 'Feel how much I want you,' he said thickly. 'Feel it, and never be scared again. You're everything I've been searching for, Emma.' His mouth rested on hers and his lips flicked delicately over her own. 'If I go on holding you like this, we'll have our wedding night ahead of time!'

With a gasp she pulled free of him, face scarlet, eyes glowing, but he would not let her escape properly, and kept his hands on her shoulders.

'Marry me?'

'Yes, yes, yes!' she cried.

'Thank God for that.' He gave a heartfelt sigh. 'At last I've got myself a permanent cook!'

Emma laughed. 'What about dinner tonight? Do we throw it out?'

'Perish the thought! In half an hour there'll be several car loads arriving from London. And I've also arranged for your grandparents to be collected and brought here.'

'How did you——'

'Pam,' he explained. 'She's been my detective and

helper.' His mouth quirked. 'So that gives us thirty minutes to make plans for our future.'

Emma had no need to ask what those plans were. The warmth of his mouth told her the story; and she knew that when the final chapters came to be written, they would have nothing to do with her cooking!

Harlequin® Plus

A HOLIDAY HAVEN

When vacation time rolls around, most people conjure up images of golden beaches, exciting nightlife and picturesque countryside. Add to this a turquoise sea, brilliant sunshine, a taste of history and a touch of the exotic...and you come up with Majorca, the setting of *A Temporary Affair*.

Majorca (or Mallorca in Spanish) is the largest of the Baleares, a group of islands in the western Mediterranean, east of Spain and north of Africa. With its rich and varied culture combining Spanish and North African influences, Majorca offers the visitor a rewarding mixture of the traditional and the modern.

Most tourists arrive—by plane or boat—at the bustling port of Palma, Majorca's modern capital. Away from this glamorous center, the adventurous visitor can seek out architectural treasures and nature's wonders, such as the stunning precipitous cliffs of the north, and the spectacular stalagmite caves and subterranean lakes in the less rugged hills of the southeast. One famous island landmark for the true romantic is the abandoned monastery at Valldemosa, where famous lovers Frédéric Chopin and George Sand once lived.

Many of the island residents carry on the life-styles of their ancestors, the farmers in particular. Some of the terraces on the higher mountain slopes, where oranges, vegetables and olives grow, date back a thousand years!

Little wonder that scenic Majorca, with its ideal climate and rich heritage, is a traveler's paradise!

PASSIONATE!

CAPTIVATING!

SOPHISTICATED!

Harlequin Presents...

The favorite fiction of women the world over!

Beautiful contemporary romances that touch every emotion of a woman's heart—passion and joy, jealousy and heartache... but most of all... love.

Fascinating settings in the exotic reaches of the world—
from the bustle of an international capital to the paradise of a tropical island.

All this and much, much more in the pages of

Wherever paperback books are sold, or through
Harlequin Reader Service

In the U.S.	In Canada
1440 South Priest Drive	649 Ontario Street
Tempe, AZ 85281	Stratford, Ontario N5A 6W2

No one touches the heart of a woman quite like Harlequin!

The bestselling epic saga of the Irish. An intriguing and passionate story that spans 400 years.

FIRST...

The Defiant

Lady Elizabeth Hatton, highborn Englishwoman, was not above using her position to get what she wanted ...and more than anything in the world she wanted Rory O'Donnell, the fiery Irish rebel. But it was an alliance that promised only ruin....

THEN...

The Survivors

Against a turbulent background of political intrigue and royal corruption, the determined, passionate Shanna O'Hara searched for peace in her beloved but troubled Ireland. Meanwhile in England, hot-tempered Brenna Coke fought against a loveless marriage....

Harlequin Romance
Man of Power
MARY WIBBERLEY
Harlequin Romance
The Winds of Winter
SANDRA FIELD
Harlequin Romance
The Leo Man
REBECCA STRATTON
Harlequin Romance
Love Beyond Reason
KAREN VAN DER ZEE
4
FREE
Harlequin Romances